2311

THE
VISITOR

Bülent Atacan

CHAPTER 1

1 B.C. Jerusalem

As a result of the changing season, the temple's huge plane trees had begun to drop their leaves on the ground. A sixteen-year-old girl was sweeping the courtyard. She was wearing a dress patched casually and a long-ragged headscarf down to her waist covering her hair partly.

After the sweeping, she was going to fetch water from the well and help in the kitchen. On the other hand, her stomach growling had already exhausted her. Even though she had had breakfast a short time ago, she was craving dates now. In recent days, her appetite had increased strangely. Suddenly, her stomach contractions became intense. No matter how hard she tried to suppress insistent reflexive heaves, remains of breakfast from her stomach lay on the ground.

First, she crouched down. Then she sat on the ground just like that. She was breathless. She gasped for air not lifting her head for some time. Later, she wiped her mouth on the end of her skirt and stood up slowly. What was this? Had she gotten a cold? She frowned while she was tucking her hair back into the headscarf. The thin line on her forehead became clear. Did that happen because something she had eaten had upsetted her stomach?

She put the scarf on her head tightly and tied a stronger knot this time. She gazed at the ground, putting her hands on her hips in exhaustion. There was no doubt she had to clean up this mess, even though she didn't have a clue why she had thrown up in the first place. She bent down and gathered some dirt and sweepings, and then spreaded them over the vomit. She repeated this action until it was covered completely.

While getting up from the ground she shivered with a soft breeze. She felt that she wasn't alone. Silence had taken over the place. Even the swallows were quiet. There was something strange going on and she could not make any sense of it. She gave an uneasy look at the temple gate and its windows. Then she took a look at the pillars and the terrace in a flash...She was alarmed with the breeze turning into a whispering strong wind, especially when it started dragging

3

what she had swept earlier. Dry leaves took off, rising up forming whirlwinds, then all of a sudden, they landed all over on the courtyard. She held her skirt with one hand and her headscarf with the other, turning her back to the wind. She squinted. Dust had gotten into her eyes. She tried to have a clear view of her surroundings. The wind had finally stopped and she was able to view the plane trees, a maple tree and a birch tree behind them. She had a sense that somebody was watching her. She took a quick look behind the temple walls. She saw something among the branches of a plane tree. She tried to open her eyes wider but her eyes hurt. She tried again after wiping her eyes with the back of her hand. This time she looked at the same spot attentively. There was a bald head with a halo over it.

She was petrified. Although she looked into the light carefully, she could not see much more than a head, which was hardly visible because of the brightness. In fact, the only thing she could see clearly was a pair of eyes. The face looked like a man's and the horrifying part was that he did not have a body. The head was floating in the air. How could this be possible? While fear spread all over her body, she was getting goose bumps on the back of her neck. The head floating between the branches of a defoliated plane tree was definitely without a body. At close range, it was impossible for her to be mistaken.

Tens of thoughts crossed over her mind in seconds. She remembered what had happened on the riverbank the other day. When she went there to do the laundry, she had come across the village women. She had rushed happily to be near them so as to be included in their conversations. As always, Mother Fatimah was sitting in the shade of a birch tree eating dates and talking to her daughters, daughters-in-law, and other young women. Mother Fatimah always had a story to tell them. When she saw Mary looking at her hungrily, she had offered her a date and Mary had accepted and eaten it despite her embarrassment.

From out of nowhere, the old woman started complaining about her daughters' and daughters-in-laws'laziness: "You are sluggish like when jinns touch gold!" she hollered and laughed out loud. When she noticed Mary's uncomprehending looks, she started telling strange stories about King Solomon's jinns. While Mary was doing the laundry, she had listened to her stories with interest like everyone else.

According to one of the stories, these jinns, who moved ten times faster than humans, had completed the construction of King Solomon's temple in a very short time. However, when these creatures touched gold, they began moving slowly like turtles. Mary didn't know jinns could communicate with humans, and therefore it was hard for her to believe what she had just heard.

She showed respect to the old woman as everyone did. For this reason, she had listened to her without opposition, leaving her doubts aside.

Now, she wished to doubt so badly at the temple courtyard, sweating bullets, cowering and trying not to collapse. She was willing that this bodiless thing would be just part of a dream she was having at that moment. That day, Mary had imagined them different; small creatures that looked like humans. What else had the old woman told about them? Like people, they had the good and the bad among them. If this was a jinn, was this a good or a bad one?

Suddenly, stories of witches with tails came to her mind. Those horrible witches that went into homes by climbing down the chimneys and eating babies' guts at nighttime. But her elder daughter-in-law had told these stories, not Mother Fatimah, and the old woman had interrupted her story saying no one had ever seen them. Although Mary did not really believe those stories, they had scared her. She even had tried hard not to think about them before bedtime. Unfortunately, she was not able to escape from a nightmare with tailed, ugly, green-faced creatures that night.

Could all those stories be real? Were they haunting her because she doubted? Was that a witch that she saw? But this creature did not have a tail and also didn't even have a body. Didn't they say they came out at night? Now, it was daytime and there wasn't a baby around at the temple… what would a witch do here? Then this had to be some jinn. But… she wondered what a jinn would look like. She regretted not asking this to Mother Fatimah that day.

While her thoughts were chasing each other, her worries turned into fear, but she couldn't stop looking at that creature. She stood seemingly nailed to the ground, standing still, confused, and looking at his eyes. This face, this baldhead… Was he confused too? Was this possible? Was he surprised that she had seen him, or the way she was staring at him? She wondered if she was being rude by staring at him. She was totally confused.

She was finally able to move. She wiped her sweaty hands on her skirt. Then she rubbed her eyes. That face was still floating there. When she came to her senses, she closed her eyes and began murmuring something. If these stories were real…even if she had to confront him, she shouldn't have done this before taking shelter in God's mercy.

She was praying, her eyes closed. Then a sudden, loud, smashing noise startled her.

"Mary, run, hurry!"

She opened her eyes and looked at the temple instinctively, recognized the voice and felt relieved.

"I'm coming," she said, wobbling.

She felt as if she had woken up from a nightmare. The fear that had permeated her body was fading away slowly. She put an indistinct

7

smile on her face. These hallucinations must have been a part of dust and sand that got into my eyes, she thought. She was an ordinary, simple girl. She wasn't an important person like King Solomon. Why would jinns come into her sight? Besides, hadn't Mother Fatimah implied that witches were superstition? She was certainly influenced by the things told that day. Or who knows, maybe she was just sick. Anyway, hadn't she thrown up couple of minutes ago? Besides that, there were those nightmares. She wondered if she had fever. Were these hallucinations and confusions because of the fever she had? Whatever the reason was, that thing she saw couldn't have been real.

She summoned up her courage and slowly turned her head back to the spot where she was looking a little while ago. As she hoped, there was nothing there but a couple of branches and leaves. The indistinctiveness left in its place a look of relief on her face. She closed her eyes one more time and thanked God with all her heart.

CHAPTER 2

YEAR 2311

He was floating naked in the air. He did not have any hair on his body and his height was approximately 6;5 ft. He was slim compared to his height. He had pale skin, blue eyes, a pointed nose, and small ears. His arms, fingers, and toes were thin and long. He was an athletic human type with wide shoulders resembling the typical anatomy of the 24th century. His body age appeared thirty-five. But his birth certificate displayed he was 155.

He was waiting for sunrise. His face turned to the horizon, he started counting down silently from ten. Finally, the first sun ray caught his eye when the count reached zero. He had memorized the exact time and place the sun would rise. He took strange pleasure from the day's first sunbeams dazzling his eyes. Squinting when this first day light danced its way through his eye lashes was a pleasant way of starting his day. In his opinion, it made a dull or an ordinary day livable this way. He had managed a program that was coordinated with earth's rotation speed, allowed his 415th floor apartment's view moving up and down for seven seconds so that first sun ray would fall with the same angle. This way, he would feel he had stopped time for seven seconds. He could freeze the sun ray as if they were on the same location for seven seconds. His byxroid dog had warned his human by barking at the 7th second.

If he wanted, with his communication device PYXOM he could extend the sun rise period for five more seconds by starting from above, but this seven second ritual was satisfying for him.

"That's it, Marco," he said bending and padding his jack russell terrier byxroid dog. He had given it this name because he was inspired by Marco Polo, an important person in history. He had named his first dog Toss. Toss was a bulldog. However, he always felt there was something missing in his relationship with Toss. Though all the character analyses showed that he could get along best with a bulldog breed. Now he had Marco and he thought he had made a good decision by listening to his 6th sense while adopting him.

"What a wonderful harmony, a wonderful friend," he said. Marco looked at Ben and wagged his tail as if he agreed.

Then, while reversing the naked vision zooming 1/300 to normal, he noticed an odd glowing. An abnormal stretch had taken place in his view.

This is not a good sign, he thought. He tried again, but the same thing happened.

"Room," he said. All of a sudden, he found himself in his room, white walls surrounding his naked body in the air.

" GISSI," he said after that. There was a disk-shaped white KRYXO underneath his feet and there came out an elastic and slippery fabric that gripped his ankles. Right after that the fabric started climbing up his legs like ivy. Soon it covered his body except his head. His halo-shaped communication device PYXOM came out of KRYXO and glided upward, passing his back and finally stopping over his head. It became active at once and started expanding at a width of two wide-open arms spreading white light. Soon after, this light became brighter. While the expanding halo was moving down his shoulders it turned into a blue color and continued its action until it became a cylindrical shape uniting with the circular KRYXO underneath his feet. This process had taken less than a second.

The blue light wall later turned into a big blue screen. He was at the riverside. He took two steps into the water. Then with his right hand he reached inside the water, he picked a stone, lifted it up and placed it on his palm carefully. He made two short and one long strike to another stone using the one in his hand. He straightened

11

up, releasing the stone. Then he reached up to the specific branch on his right and pulled it downwards. At that moment it was decoded. The river view vanished and there appeared many screens around him.

"I sometimes have difficulty understanding myself. Very few PYXOM users put passwords on their screens. I have nothing to hide or no secret information to keep. Then why do I have it? Whatever," he said, leaving his thoughts behind.

In a fast mode of hand gestures, eye blinks, and speech techniques that could not be followed by an ordinary person, he interacted with the screens.

"Eye test," he said. Little lights started flashing on the left and right. The lights projected from the center, scanning his eye and the light screen. It was bad news. Scanning detected an eye deformation. A new eye request was submitted for his consent.

> 1/300 optics Click
> Color: Same Click
> Shape: Same Click
> Apply: Click

The new eye transplantation would be available in two months. There was nothing else for him to do about this, but wait.

Then, on his screen he saw the titles waiting to be voted for the CLES (Communal Living

Engagement System) that was broadcast by the commune council. At the same time, he had a conversation request. This was Ellie. In this case, he could postpone the voting.

He accepted Ellie's virtual meeting right away. She had picked a walnut tree shade by the lake for a meeting place. While Ellie preferred nature, Ben always picked a historical site. She was sitting in one of the armchairs in the shade, waiting for him. Ben placed himself in the opposite armchair. This was one of the weekly routine meetings that didn't have an agenda. They had known each other for more than twenty years. Their interaction had started in a conversation group and later this had turned into private meetings. Since then, they did not accept anyone else in their meetings.

"How have you been lately?" asked Ellie, her legs crossed, sitting, her back straight and her green eyes not looking at him directly and rather in a shy way. She always looked at him shy and tilting her head slightly. She had a wide forehead and large cheekbones. Her dimples became visible when she smiled. She was an elegant woman. She was one hundred and fifty years old but she looked thirty-five because of the mutation she had.

How come she looks like her great- great grandmother this much? thought Ben

Ellie was petting her byxroid cat delicately on her lap. Her cat had short gray fur and big, shiny, yellow eyes. Her name was Pearl. She was independent and very smart. This Burmese cat was staring at Ben. Then Pearl started moving her head from side to side, looking for Marco. Irritated by Pearl's looks, without Ellie noticing, Ben called Marco and had him sit on his lap, activating his holomex image. Thereupon, Pearl directed her looks at Marco and moved her tail up and down slowly showing her pleasure. Marco replied by wagging his tail. He got up from where he was sitting and sat at the edge of the armchair. Then they looked at one another. They had known each other for a long time and got along well. Ben knew the reason why Ellie had brought Pearl to their meeting. This meant Ellie wanted a long conversation with Ben and he liked this. He was obsessed by the way she sat in that armchair. Despite how she sat looked familiar, there was something he couldn't figure out. He thought he had seen this way of sitting and posture somewhere else. But where?

It must have been a long break of silence before he felt Ellie turn her head and look at him with curiosity.

Thereupon, he rested his arms on his armchair, making himself comfortable

"Johann Strauss," he said referring to the background music

"OK. Which composition?"

"Just a second," he said and concentrated on the music.

"Isn't it Blue Danube Waltz?"

"You did not cheat, did you?" She turned to Ben throwing him a naughty look.

"My favorite in classical music is Amadeus Mozart," said Ben and added, "I seldom listen to waltzes."

"Ben, you know what I'm thinking? We, as a commune gave necessary importance to technology, but on the other hand we ignored art and music."

"Hearing this from you is surprising."

"The places we live are all plain and have light colors. Don't you think this a little dull?"

"I've never thought about it in this respect. Yes, a little change would be nice."

"What about the colors and patterns on our GISSIs. Wouldn't it be nice to see the patterns of creative artists on us giving a magic touch to our lives?"

Ben thought Ellie couldn't escape her female instincts, despite her mutation.

"We should organize memorial days at certain times."

"Mm," said Ben, doubting.

"A waltz night, for instance."

"You mean, are we going to dance like in the old times? I can't even imagine this."

"Why not?"

"I don't even know how to dance."

"We would learn."

"If we were dancing now, most probably, I would have stepped on your foot a dozen times or maybe more."

"Why did you say that?"

"I have eye deformation."

"It's been thirty years since the last transplant. I need the fifth eye transplantation," said Ben.

Ellie squinted. She nodded as if saying," I see."

"Time goes so fast," she said. Then she straightened her head and became silent, closing her eyes.

Although he had known Ellie for a long time, he still found her mysterious. Perhaps she was hiding or not telling him something. Ben spent his every second trying to analyze her. He wondered if she was trying to analyze him, too. Had she sensed his feelings and thoughts for her? Was she trying to make sense of his behavior down to the last detail?

If she was in such effort, she must have solved me already, he thought. Time to time, he felt that Ellie was already aware of everything. He wasn't wrong about this. All in all, he was not dealing with an ordinary person. She was the most successful Professor Dimension of the commune. She was known as a genius in the scientific department. She described herself as a listener of symphony of universe. She gave the names of musical instruments to the dimensions she explored, and said her goal was to bring out the hidden conductor in her. She had been successful in gaining everybody's attention and admiration.

Her only virtue wasn't her impressive statements, of course. The most admiration came from her achievements that marked an era. Before her explorations, travels to ancient times only consisted of silent images. She had pulled out noise flexes from the depths of space that had fallen behind light speed and had synchronized them with light. It was her formulas that united image and sound for the first time. Ben had heard about her success for the first time with this achievement and had joined her conversation group in order to know her better.

Moreover, when they first started having these personal meetings Ben had asked her why she continued seeing him and what her expectations were.

"History," Ellie had answered. "Knowing the past is a gate to future."

Then, she had asked the same question to Ben.

"Mystery of future," Ben had answered.

Neither of them had scrutinized the answers they received. Ben had actually meant the mystery of her. That was all he wanted to explore. He had regretted not asking her what she meant by her answer. Because he didn't want to look obsessed, he hadn't brought up the subject. Actually, solving her mystery had become an obsession for him. He was spending his free time traveling to the past, looking into her background.

"You didn't comment on my eye transplantation," said Ben, finally. He just wanted to say something to slow down his thoughts.

"Oh, yes. You're lucky!"

"Lucky?"

"Of course. Eye transplantation is pretty easy. We are still unable to change one organ you know," she said.

"Couldn't the brain transplantation committee make any progress?"

"Unfortunately, there is no new development. The functioning of the brain is a lot different than any other organ. You know that we were able to overcome the issues with the sense of smell and emotions. On the other hand, on the subject of genes, the communication between them is very complicated. Moreover, there are risks. For instance, we can remove your brain and transplant it to another body, but we can't prevent the risks during this process. As you see, it's very dangerous. We still need more time and effort to make progress."

"Why is it dangerous?"

"The brain is an organ that has a very strong interaction with its own environment. It's in a continuous communication with the sources it provides nutrition to and keeps a record for each communication. You see, we haven't been able to delete these records yet. Danger for human generation emerges here. In the future, there is a chance that brains created for humans might get under the control of byxroids because they would be the products of the same artificial environment. Growing a brain in a natural environment brings a living status to it constitutionally. On the other hand, there isn't a handicap for the other organs. As you see, this subject matter is pretty sophisticated. Therefore, there are a lot of problems to overcome. Yet, if we break the brain down into particles, compress them in high density and create a spiral moving on the same wavelength, then there won't be any need for a physical body."

She looked at Ben's eyes, hesitating that she was dwelling on this subject way too much. But when she saw he was listening with interest, she continued.

"Think. No gravity, no oxygen dependency, no toxin discharge, no need to get into REST every eight hours. Even if we add more fiction into it... If a line of light beam traveling between X and Y is created and along this line if we accelerate the neutrinos, do you think we would be able to go beyond the stabilized light speed barrier?

"To tell the truth I am not familiar with this subject, so I can't even imagine this. It sounds like fiction to me," said Ben and then asked,

"Well, how long will it take to accomplish this? What do you think?"

"I don't know. This is just a theory. Currently, there are also studies about the use of frexes of a black hole's gravitational force to create a stream of photons. There is an associate professor named Naochi who is only twenty-five and has already made progress on this field.

"Twenty-five? So, he hasn't had any organ transplantations yet?"

"Yes. No one from Science society opposed to Naochi's hypothesis of light beams caught by black hole and these beams bending like they are jammed in a clamp and the light becoming a part of the mass and as a result, the energy value occurs during this process would be equal to the infinity in the pi number.

"Interesting,"

"Anyway, if I get back to what I was saying, even though it's important, the energy transfer theory between those two points has not been totally developed yet. For instance, one of the important subjects that must be accomplished is a form of communication that will be set up by an energy spiral. How will this communication be? One way maybe?

"Wait a second," said Ben. "The subject is a little deviating here. When you say communication, does that include the dimension after death? "

Although his voice was calm, his expression on his face showed he was excited and perhaps a little confused.

"Yes," said Ellie, smiling. "I know this sounds impossible. But we think it's possible to carry this off. Theoretically there hasn't been a frame formed for this yet. But, I can't resist the fascination of this. It is pulling me in so badly… It's almost like an obsession." After a short pause, she continued.

"I nearly spend most of my free time on this subject. Even so, there is no specification on this.

I think my obsession could be excused since there are so many unknowns waiting to be analyzed. You see, this is the most mysterious subject to me: Death."

She had almost whispered when she said the last word. Then she kept quiet for some time, watching the scenery across the lakeshore. There appeared a faint smile on her lips. She was as if looking at something that Ben couldn't see. At last, she took a deep breath while shaking her head left to right like she was trying to get rid of something in her mind. She turned to Ben again.

"It's exciting, right?" asked her eyes, sparkling

"It really is. Compelling at the same time," said Ben, sighing. By this, he hadn't only implied what Ellie had told him, but his situation as well. In order not to reveal what had crossed his mind, he added right after this, "I mean what you told me...it appears so."

"Absolutely," said Ellie. She was so fascinated by her own words that she didn't realize Ben's sudden mood change.

"Because this is a compelling subject, groups of twelve experts in different fields who make their own research on death and after death join the committee continuously. Our number has reached 540. Figure the communication traffic between us. Recently, we tried to prevent the dispersion of frex waves and the energy at the time of death. Well, at the same time, we sought ways of capturing and keeping this energy in a certain space. If you like I can manage to have you accepted into our group as an observer. Well, of course, if you are interested in observing how the energy disperses from the organism at the moment of death and how it is sucked by the universe."

"Actually, you know, I am pretty busy nowadays. I shouldn't be distracted, but…"
He paused. He was encountering a new puzzle piece, right when he thought he knew Ellie so well. Lately, he had been thinking of her every minute, trying to figure her out.

However, he had questions in his mind that he couldn't find answers to. If he had to watch the death of an organism for this, he would do it with pleasure. After calculating what to say, he started speaking with a smile on his face.

"I sure am. It's hard for me to be indifferent to what you have told me. As soon as I am relieved from my busy schedule--"
Ben could not complete his sentence because a message had appeared on his screen. Ellie also had received a message. They both concentrated on it for a few seconds. Then, they looked at each other.

"A reminder," said Ben smiling.

"Yes, mine is too," said Ellie, "Then see you in ten minutes."

Ben nodded and their meeting ended.

CHAPTER 3

"Asking permission for REST filling," said a soft voice in the apartment. Those peaceful minutes had vanished in an instant.

"What time is it?" Ben asked reluctantly.

"9:52:15," said the voice.

"Permitted. Apartment display."

In no time, the surroundings turned into a room with white floors, white ceilings, and white walls. REST was one of the limited devices that commune people used in their daily life. It was in a shape of a transparent sphere. Mutant people got rid of their harmful toxins by getting into these spheres. At the same time, it provided daily body cleansing, body rest, and necessary minerals, protein, and vitamins. This treatment had to be applied for ten minutes, every eight hours. Two human-looking byxroids got inside and quickly moved toward the REST device.

Byxroids were second-generation artificial humans. Compared to Byxbots, the first version,

Byxroids were more productive, functional, and more sophisticated. Their mission was to carry out the commands. Their risk of doing wrong was almost zero percent and their calculation speed was a lot higher compared to humans. The idea developing and decision-making mechanisms found in Byxbots were bordered and decreased in Byxroids because shortly after their manufacture, Byxbots had established a communication line between them. At first, the commune welcomed this development.

Moreover, Byxbots had started enhancing their IQ levels by themselves. They also developed devices with different functions, made decisions on their own and had manufacturing without any notifications or consultation of the commune. This had disturbed the commune. Byxbots were given earthquake prevention job. The job location was at the elastic layer, seven miles under the earth surface. At that depth, they created a lot of big gaps using the devices they manufactured and again they did not inform the commune. These huge gaps had canals reaching the earth surface and they had nothing to do with the earthquake prevention project. The commune came to the conclusion that the Byxbots' secret acts had become a current issue. This situation meant uncertainty and obscurity for not only the commune but also for humanity. The commune perceived this as a threat and therefore put the Byxbot manufacture aside. Now, second generation Byxroids were dealing with daily routine jobs. The only difference that distinguished a byxroid from a human was the little star at the back of their neck and an ID card the size of an eye placed under it.

While one of the byxroids was getting into the device, the other checked the device functions. Then, the feeding cartridge was replaced with a new one and toxin wastes were emptied. After that, the byxroids left the apartment as they came, not looking around.

"What time is it?"

"9:54:27"

I still have six minutes to the appointment, he thought. It would take him maximum forty seconds to get down to the kids' floor from his 415th floor.

"FRYXO," he called.

His FRYXO had arrived from the vehicle storage after twenty seconds. Although he still had five minutes, he didn't want to wait. He moved forward to his sphere-shaped vehicle in the corner of the room. The door opened. The KRYXO underneath his feet first expanded backward, and then upward. Next, it transformed into a seat. After Ben sat and felt the suction on his back, it turned slightly sideways and got into the FRYXO. The door closed.

"Children's floor," said Ben.

In the meantime, the outer space KX3 type observatory was operating in the invisible exterior mode. It was doing its routine work, transmitting the data obtained from the outer space to the main operating base on Earth. It was observing the activities of the closest black hole, twenty-three light years from Earth. The black hole was absorbing the gases of stars by forming spiral-shaped disks. The observatory was monitoring this process using the Ner 3 rays.

Suddenly, the control room lights in the observatory turned red. This situation indicated an abnormality. It meant danger. The source of the alert was detected in no time. There had been an unusual activity in the black hole. This was reported to the main base right away.

CHAPTER 4

The cover underneath his FRYXO opened and the connection corridor to the main tunnel appeared. After waiting three seconds for a secure passage, the vehicle mingled with other FRYXOs and started moving downward. While most of the vehicles were going toward the tunnels that went out of the building, Ben went forward directly to the ground floor. Soon the vehicle stopped, the door opened and after his seat turned slightly, it carried him out. His seat transformed into a disk while he was straightening up. Now he was standing on his KRYXO.

Kate, who was in charge of child development center, was there to meet him virtually. Kate was a young black woman having a curved shape proportional body.

"Hello, I am Kate. You are early, Ben," she said.

Ben nodded.

"I can accompany you and Ellie five minutes later. While you are in the waiting room, I can display some of your childhood memories on your screen if you wish."

"That will be great. Thank you," said Ben.

The woman smiled and then her holomex disappeared suddenly. Ben had just begun to move but he stopped when he saw a FRYXO approaching. It was Ellie. He watched Ellie preparing to get out of her vehicle. She was filled with grace. While watching her, he felt as if time had slowed down. His eyes had been locked on her movements. He watched her every move carefully while she was approaching him. At that moment, he was filled with desire to touch her. He extended his hand as soon as she came near him. But Ellie pretended not to see this; as usual she turned down his help and gave him a courtly smile.

Ben tried to hide his embarrassment when she came out of her vehicle. Her seat transformed into a disk that later on went under her feet. Ellie's GISSI colors and patterns reflected her mood. It covered her body with yellow, orange and gray stripes.

"You're early," said Ellie.

"Yes, you, too. We will be taken care of five minutes later. I was just going to watch my childhood memories to kill time. Would you like to join me?

"Sure, why not."

She had just completed her sentence when Kate's holomex appeared between Ben and Ellie.

"Hello. I am Kate. I can join you and Ben in four minutes. While you are in the waiting room, I can display some of your childhood memories on your screen if you wish."

"Of course," said Ellie and as soon as Kate's holomex disappeared, Ellie and Ben caught each other's eye.

"I can't believe we are here," said Ellie, while moving toward the waiting room.

"Me, too," said Ben smiling and trying to leave behind his embarrassment moments.

"If we can accomplish this procedure, we will spend a lot of time here," he added and then he turned and looked at her with silence. Later, he said, "Together," stressing the word.

"I guess so," she said with a faint smile and a quick glance at Ben.

Why are you so mysterious, Ellie? he thought. He was captivated by his curiosity again. He had to solve the mystery of her. But how?

"How is school going?" asked Ellie with a timid tone. She seemed to be trying to change the subject.

Before Ben answered, his KRYXO had transformed into an armchair, changing its disk form. They had arrived at the waiting room. They felt the vacuums behind their back and when they rested their arms on the armchair, they took off and moved away from each other. His childhood memories display started flowing before his eyes, his babyhood, his mom and dad, his birthdays and his mischief on his 8th birthday. Instead of watching his memories that he had watched many times before, he was carefully eying Ellie who was watching her childhood memories. She had that faint smile on her face once again.

A ten-year-old dark-haired boy had appeared on the wide screen in front of her. This was Gabe. Ellie had golden hair at that time.

"Come on, give me a high five!" said the boy to this golden-haired girl, raising his one arm.

Little Ellie didn't know what he meant by this. She just looked at him surprised. Then, she hesitantly raised her arm as well.

"Why are we doing this?" she asked.

"You'll understand," said Gabe.

As soon as Ellie lowered her arm, the boy said: "High five!"

It was obvious that she didn't make sense out of this game, but she gave him a high five anyway.

"What is going on, Gabe? Why are we doing these high fives?" she asked curiously.

"You'll understand," he said and winked at her.

After a short confusion, her eyes glowed and then she smiled. She turned to Gabe excitedly, as if something had come to her mind. This time she held her arm up and said:

"High five!"

Gabe responded to her high five with a big smile and then asked:

"What happened? What for now?"

"You'll understand," said Ellie and this time she winked at him.

"I see that it didn't take you long to understand," said Gabe and they both started laughing.

Then the images on the screen changed. She started watching the joke she played on Gabe and Xane during a lesson at school. She was sitting between them. First, Ellie poked Xane's arm and then whispered in her ear:

"Gabe is going to tell you something."

After this, she turned to Gabe who was following the lesson.

"Xane is calling you," she whispered into Gabe's ear.

Right after that, she backed off by leaning back in her seat and started watching the two. Shortly after Gabe and Xane looked at each other, they started using gestures and signs to make themselves understood by one another. While Ellie was sitting in between she watched them gesturing and signing. At the same time, she tried to hide the naughty smile on her face. After, Gabe and Xane gestured for quite some time; they got tired of it and leaned back in their seats.

Ellie was quietly giggling, covering her mouth with her hand.

Then, her eight-year-old image was on the screen. She was in a class again and their mentor was asking the same question to every one.

"Whom do you want to be loved by the most? Your mom or dad?"

"My dad," said Ellie smiling.

The mentor asked the same question to Gabe who was sitting next to Ellie.

"Neither of them. I want God to love me the most," said Gabe.

His unexpected answer had surprised everyone. He was very smart and very independent at the same time. He liked being naughty. Had he said that because that was naughty of him and he wanted attention or was he sincere in his answer? This question was answered when Gabe became twelve and took his place among the Believers as Gabriel.

Ellie thought how wonderful those days were while watching her childhood memories. She really used to get along with Gabe so well. They hadn't seen each other for a long time and she had missed him so much. She decided to go to holy land as soon as she was done that day.

The images on their screens disappeared when their waiting time was over. Ben thought he should spend more time with Ellie while they were getting close to each other. Fortunately, he had a good reason for this.

After a while they came side by side and Kate entered the waiting room. She came close and then stopped right before them. She sat down when her KRYXO transformed into an armchair.

"Hello and welcome to our children's world," she said with an affectionate smile.

Ellie and Ben smiled back at her.

"First of all, I'd like to congratulate you as a result of your decision. I am very excited that you have undertaken a very important mission, which will add value to our humanity by bringing a new person to our world. During this period, I would like you to know that, I will need your self-devotion and love for this baby. We will ask you to spare two hours a day for the baby. Of course, we will be with you all the time during those hours. You should have no doubts that we will provide you with any kind of help and support when you request. I suppose you know the procedure. I am aware that you still have time for your final decision. It's very kind of you to visit us instead of communicating with your PYXOMs. I'd like to thank you for this. Please do not hesitate if you have any questions to ask me. I will be pleased to answer them.

Ben and Ellie looked at one another for some time. For a few seconds they thought if they had any questions, but they didn't. This wasn't going to be a natural giving birth. The reason they were there was to be a mentor for the baby in a psychological way, not to learn about child nutrition or education.

"You had said you wanted to observe the children instead of making direct contact with them. To tell the truth, I wonder why you came here, although you didn't need to," said Kate with an affectionate smile on her face.

"Actually, we changed our minds," said Ben.

"We wanted to feel the ambience here."

Ellie nodded, "And I want to make direct contact with them," she added.

"Sightseeing Tour," said Kate in a soft tone.

Right after this, both Ellie and Ben commanded at the same time: "Follow!"

Their armchairs moved slowly into the air. Following Kate, they went through a big light screen that looked like a wall. Then all of a sudden, they found themselves in a beautiful grove full of colorful flowers and various trees. They could hear the birds chirping. In the middle, there was a yard. There were about twenty children aged between three and four and they were running and playing joyfully on the green grass.

"I can't see any toys," said Ellie to Ben.

"Yes," said Kate when she heard Ellie.

"This is the time period for them to focus on each other, to socialize, and to develop their ability to communicate without using any devices. This period plays a significant role in their future lives. They are learning to be able to keep their emotions under control and be motivated to do this. This is the period when children are the most peaceful and therefore there have been continuous efforts to increase this time period."

At that moment a little girl left the group and ran toward Ellie. She stopped right before her and smiled.

"Hello," she said and reached out to touch Ellie.

"May I touch?" the little girl asked, pointing Ellie's head. Ellie was surprised; she looked at Ben and then to Kate, not knowing what to do or how to respond. Then, she accepted her request by smiling. Ellie bent her head and the child touched her bald head and then she started patting it.

When she felt the warmness of those tender little hands on her head, Ellie smiled again. It was as if something moved inside her, and this later wrapped around her being. She felt a wave of happiness surrounding her soul, her heart filling up with pure love. She wondered where these feelings were hiding until now while she was trying to suppress the tears filling her eyes.

"What is your name?" Ellie asked.

"Emily," the little girl answered. Her eyes shone with joy.

"This is my great great grandmother's name," she said.

Then the child reached for Ellie's hand and put it on her own head. Ellie stroked the little girl's long, wavy, golden blonde hair while smiling.

"Come with me," the little girl said, holding Ellie's hand again. Ellie looked at Kate one more time. After receiving approval, she straightened up and her armchair transformed into a disk under her feet.

"Let's walk," said the little girl.

Ellie got off her KRYXO excitedly and stepped on the ground. The little girl grabbed her hand tightly this time and took Ellie to the other children. They formed a circle all together and started turning. Hearing the children's laughter had cheered her up so much that she began laughing with them joyfully. She hadn't felt this peaceful and she was happier than ever before while the sky above her head spun round and round. She was flooded with emotions and there was no way to keep them under control.
She didn't want this moment to end. She wanted to feel those little fingers in her hands, turning and turning forever.

For a moment, she caught Ben's eye. He was smiling too. Then she looked at Kate.

"Children don't have many visitors. For this reason, they got excited when they saw you," said Kate.

"Her hair---"Ellie couldn't finish her sentence when Kate interrupted.

"Their genetic mutations will take place after they are twelve and they will lose all the head and body hair then. We have to continue our tour by the way."

"I know. I was trying to say how beautiful her hair was. I used to have hair like hers when I was little," said Ellie.

"Come on, Ellie. It's time to leave," said Ben. But his unwillingness to leave could be sensed in his voice.

Ellie looked at the kids; moments ago, that careless smile on her face, that magic in the air had gone. She had stopped but the children didn't want to let go of their hands, especially the little girl on her right who had patted her head.

"I have to go, children," she said in a sad tone. She made eye contact with each one of them. Then, in order to bring her control back and to gather herself up, she took a deep breath.

"Thank you for letting me play with you. I've had a great time."

The little fingers holding her hand loosened.

"Will you come again?" the little girl asked smiling at Ellie. Ellie turned and looked at Kate.

"Sure. If you want this too," said Kate nodding.

"I will come," said Ellie facing the little girl. Then she bent down and patted her long hair while the girl patted Ellie's head.

The sound of the children's laughter moments ago had vanished. They were now standing still, watching Ellie leave. Ellie got on top of her KRYXO. It quickly transformed into an armchair. She turned around and looked at the children one more time. They were waving at her. She waved back at them.

"I'm sorry," said Ben.

Ellie looked at him with a bitter smile for a while. Then she closed her eyes and sighed. Later on, they left the place going through another light screen wall.

Here was a group of children between five and six who were overwhelmed with excitement trying to pick a water train track. Five children sat on the seats next to each other. A water-screen in the shape of a box underneath them started to rise with the train wagon while evaporating. When the train wagon rose to 150 feet, the water bent downward and the wagon moved with it. Then it switched to a free fall. When they were about to hit the ground, kids started screaming and suddenly the water screen bent upward. The wagon made a spin and then started climbing up once again. This time it had risen to 200 feet.

"Excuse me," Kate said and moved fast toward the train wagon. The children had climbed up to 100 feet. Kate followed them up on her KRYXO.

"Down!" said Kate.

As soon as she said that, the train wagon started descending and finally landed on the grass. While the children were getting off the train unwillingly, Kate had arrived there. All the children stood, their heads bowed in shame as they knew what they did was wrong. Kate gave them the eye and then got back to the others.

"They are a handful at this age. They don't have limits; they don't know where to stop. I wish we could predict their next move and prevent their wrong doing," said Kate smiling.

Ellie nodded. She was quiet and looked as if she was lost in her thoughts. Anyone could tell that she was far away from where she was.

They left that place and moved on to another section. There were seven-year-old children here. They were learning the enhanced alphabet. A byxroid was telling the children the meanings of the shapes and the colors inside them that were popping up in the air.

"Yes, let's go over it. How many shapes are there in your alphabet?"

"Fifty," the children answered altogether.

"Correct. There are also eleven colors and thirty-five letters. Is that right children?"

"Yes," they said altogether again.

"Which color is the most important and refers to danger?"

"Brown," said the children.

"Very good. The male and female shapes that have an "I" letter in it represent you. All right," the byxroid said. Then, a white circle with letter "I" in it popped up on top of their heads.

"What does white represent?"

"Emotions," they answered.

"Excellent, outstanding!" said the byxroid."

"Grayish whites express unhappiness, yellowish ones excitement, reddish ones anxiety, and the greenish ones express our happiness. Well, you know these very well already, don't you?"

"Yes!" said the children.

"OK, when we open this letter," the byxroid said and gave a signal. Right after the signal, there appeared a line of shapes, colors and letters under the letter" I".

"When we examine the letter in detail, we will see all the recorded information about you."

Ben thought that alphabet had gone through so many phrases since the Phoenicians and he remembered how he had learned the old and the common alphabet at his grandfather's time. Just then, his eye caught Ellie. She was watching the children but she seemed far off. He wished he could read her mind at that moment.

"Shall we go on?"

Kate interrupted Ben's thoughts. He nodded.

"OK," said Ellie vaguely.

This time they moved in the opposite direction and went through another wall. When they reached the main lounge, they saw three men walking in their direction. They were shaggy; they had long hair and long beards and all three of them were a bit chubby and looked elderly. But their eyes were bright, filled with energy. The breeze swept through their long hair while they walked. One them were wearing a baggy, long white dress made from old school fabric. While they passed by Ellie and others, the man in the white dress caught Ellie's eye and they exchanged looks. Ellie and the man smiled at each other sincerely. Then the man greeted Ben and Kate with a head gesture. The other two men followed him and greeted them the same way.

Ben turned to Ellie wondering if she knew the man. When he saw Ellie smiling at him, his curiosity rose. Then he turned and looked at Kate with questioning eyes.

"Believers," said Kate.

"The commune that lives in holy land. They come here once a month and inform the children about beliefs."

"Interesting."

"It is. I should give them a credit for that. The hours they spend with the children are really amazing."

"I didn't know there was a passage from here to holy land," said Ben.

"The passage is closed to most communes. Even though not very often, believers are one of the communes that we have open passage to. If you are concerned about viruses, bacteria, or harmful organisms like parasites that they might bring over here, this is not possible because they are decontaminated in the quarantine room at the passing zone. But they suffer from small illnesses when they get back to their land. Anyway, there isn't a busy traffic between the two territories."

"I thought their territory was quite far from ours. I don't think it's a walking distance so how do they deal with the transportation?"

Ellie joined the conversation. "They use our FRYXOs when they are away from their land. Since FRYXO's have virus removers in them, it's pretty safe."

Ben was confused. He looked at Ellie puzzled. He wondered how she knew all about this.

"When I have time, I visit them, especially my childhood friend, Gabriel," said Ellie.

"Was your friend Gabriel one of those men whom you greeted?"

Ellie smiled. "Yes"

He was a history professor and he could travel in history, but he did not have permission for entering to the past one hundred and fifty years. The reason was the respect for private life. In order to travel to those time periods, first you had to have the approval of the commission. Second, it was possible to go on designated dates with the members of the commission only. For this reason, he knew very well that he didn't have a chance to look at Ellie's near past life. Although he was bursting with curiosity, he believed he would be able to gather the puzzle pieces in time.

While he was lost in thought, he was startled by a sudden feeling that Ellie and Kate were staring at him. He turned around.

"Shall we go on I have asked? I'm expecting an answer from you, Ben," said Kate.

"Definitely, go ahead, please."

They started following Kate and later went through another light screen wall.

They found themselves in a math class for eight-year- olds. There was a bitten apple display in the air. On the upper left side there was its ripening date, its size and time calculations and on the upper right side its chemical synthesis was on display. On the left bottom was its varied weight and gravity force values, and on the right bottom was displayed the measurements of its alteration in time. Numbers were changing all the time. Children were paying close attention to the apple.

After watching the children for a while, Kate signaled them with her head to proceed. Ben and Ellie followed her.

They were in the main lounge again. Time was up. They left Kate after they thanked her.

While they were heading to their FRYXOs, Ben said, "You look occupied."

She looked at him and her lips moved as if she was going to say something, but then she changed her mind and looked away from him. She took a deep breath and looked back at Ben. She was determined this time.

"I want a girl, not a boy," she said

Ben was very much surprised by Ellie's unexpected statement. He didn't say anything. He just stared at her; his expression was blank for some time.

"Actually, I've been thinking about it for a long time, but I couldn't tell you this. The little girl I met recently, Emily, she helped me with my indecisiveness on this matter. Now I've made my decision."

"But Ellie, after all the significant progress we made toward this, do you think it's right to change your mind now?"

His voice was calm but his eyeballs had gotten bigger and he was frowning.

"I thought you wanted a boy, too. You've never mentioned a girl until today. Even so to say…"

He took a deep breath to stay calm. Then he continued speaking with the same tone of voice.

"Until today, you acted as if the gender was not important to you. Am I wrong?"

Ellie didn't answer. She just stared at him. Ben was determined about acting calm, but yet, he was not ready to accept the decision she had made without discussing it with him.

"This is such an important issue. It is improper to decide on your own and telling me just now. This is wrong and you know it."

"I know this is so sudden, Ben. You're right. Believe me, I understand how I put you into this."

"Do you really understand?" He paused, lowering his head slightly. He looked at her for a while. He was trying to figure out what she was thinking from the expression on her face.

"To tell the truth, I must say that I doubt this a little," he added.

"Of course, I understand. You questioning me won't change anything." She looked away from him. She avoided looking at his face. Her eyes had been focused on the light screen door they had passed through with Kate a while ago. She had a decisive expression on her face.

"That I hadn't told you before, there is no way to make up for this. The only thing I can do is to tell you I am sorry for putting you in this situation. I am really sorry. But as I said before, I've made my decision." She paused and then looked at Ben this time.

"If you need some time to think about this, I understand. I think you should consider it. This is a very important matter. Let's not discuss this hastily. Maybe later… when you reach a decision, please let me know.

"Ellie…" But Ben could not continue his sentence. She was right; they didn't need to discuss this now. And it was obvious that Ellie had no intention to continue talking about the issue. Ben sighed and his shoulders sank.

She sounded serious when she said "I look forward to hearing from you," and again she looked away from him.

Although anyone could see how great his disappointment was, Ellie didn't say anything else and left the building with her FRYXO.

In the meantime, the KX3 observatory was still on red alert. All the unusual data had already been transmitted to the main base on Earth in the Ovax format. Even though this transmission was in the Ovax format, it still took some time to reach Earth. The data indicated an unknown, shiny, white tube-shaped structure slowly coming out of the black hole. Shortly after, it was out of sight as if it was never there. A similar situation had not been observed before and this wasn't a typical activity of a black hole.

When it vanished, all indicators in the observatory reverted to normal and the red lights turned off.

But this didn't last long. Shortly after that, all lights in the observatory **turned brown.** This meant the highest level of alert.

CHAPTER 5

After Ben got back home, he realized he had almost lost his control. In order to ease his mind, he had made some calls, had done some voting that had been pending for some time and had traveled to 2070 to prepare for his lesson that day. But none of these had helped him to calm down.

At the end, he decided to intervene instead of fudging the issue.

"Meditation," he called. With this command, first his KRYXO transformed into an armchair, then right after that he leaned back. When he stretched his legs, it changed into a horizontal position. As soon as he lay down, the room lights dimmed and Mozart's 40th symphony started playing.

Although he tried to fling himself into the music and ease his mind, his thoughts had taken control of him; his mood alternated between rage and heartbreak. A few minutes later, when he was filled with exhaustion, he realized meditation wouldn't work for him either, so he straightened up slowly and the music stopped. For some time, he just sat there and waited, not knowing what to do. Then, all of a sudden, he jumped to his feet like something had occurred to him. While the room was lightening, he called his FRYXO.

After reporting the coordinates and being confirmed for a safe pass, the connection corridor gate opened and his vehicle moved to the main tunnel, then to the city line, and finally moved toward the city building exit.

After a while he left the city building. He commanded his FRYXO for "Horizontal Flight Mode". The sphere-shaped vehicle widened, stretching upward and to the sides.

When Ben straightened up, his seat transformed into a disk and then it was pulled under his feet. Right after that, the front part expanded to his height by stretching upward. He felt the vacuums in front of his body. Then his KRYXO started moving slowly. Finally, it put Ben face down in a reclining position by completing a ninety-degree turn in vertical axis. In the meantime, his PYXOM appeared; it went straight to the back of his head and stayed there. From the front part of the ring a transparent protection shield came down; it covered his face on the front and sides like a glass bowl and then got connected to a flexible platform from under his chin. FRYXO's ceiling opened; its walls got pulled down and its width narrowed until it was about three feet

Ben opened his arms and commanded, "Increase the speed". Then he closed his eyes, enjoying the wind, and he moved on like this for a few seconds. Later he opened his eyes and watched the scenery.

Under him was a river, curving under the shade of trees along its shores. He looked up. There were a couple of clouds but the sky was clear and bright. There appeared a smile on his face. He looked down again and suddenly started descending. When his FRYXO's base hit the surface of the river, he put his hands into the water and moved on like this for a while. When some rocks appeared on the surface, his vehicle ascended.

Soon, he saw a waterfall flowing into the river. As soon as he commanded his vehicle to shut, his FRYXO's walls started rising on both sides and finally joined at the top. He directed his vehicle to the waterfall without hesitation. As soon as the vehicle entered the waterfall, it made a sharp upward maneuver and started to climb up in the waterfall by spinning. When it reached the top, it continued ascending. After a while, it made a sharp U turn and went into a nosedive toward the river. But it went up again before reaching the ground.

Then, suddenly, he stopped his vehicle. It floated in the air for a while. He looked around and then moved on leaving the waterfall behind him.

He had arrived at The Grand Canyon in seconds. He went back to a sitting position while he was flying between the hills. After some time wandering, he found this boring and couldn't help thinking of Ellie. He turned his vehicle toward the high hill he had just past moments ago and then he landed on the flat surface of its peak.

As soon as FRYXO's door opened, his KRYXO carried him outside and transformed into a disk under his feet. He moved toward the hillside. Then he stopped and stood on one of the rocks, and got ready to watch the scenery.

Despite all his efforts, he was back with his thoughts again and the joy he felt a short time ago had deserted him. He frowned; his lips strained and then he started watching the breathtaking scenery.

He received a reminding message from his PYXOM while he was deep in thought. The doctor was informing him about his seventh appointment that would be after eight minutes today. He looked at the message on the screen with a blank expression; he had had an appointment with the doctor just yesterday. A second appointment in twenty-four hours... This must be an emergency situation. If not, we would have scheduled a time and date before this appointment. He remembered what he and Ellie had talked about. He had been busy thinking about the issue all day long but hadn't figured out

50

the sudden change in her attitude. He had become so confused that it was almost impossible to come to a solution. And now, when he saw this reminding message, he wondered if Ellie was coming to this appointment or not. This caused him to plunge into despair and anxiety.

He finally ran out of patience and commanded his PYXOM to start the meeting. Ellie and the doctor's frozen images appeared on his screen. There was six minutes to the appointment. He forgot about the scenery and where he was. He didn't know how to kill time. He locked his eyes on his screen and waited.

A couple of minutes later, before the appointment, he sent a private meeting request to Ellie. He thought this meeting would help him get the answers to his questions. But instead, he received an automatic busy message from Ellie.

While he was thinking what to do, he received a meeting request from the doctor's office. This was Lucy. He accepted the request right away.

"Hello, Ben. Your meeting starts in two minutes. You are early. Meanwhile, can I help you with anything?" asked Lucy.

"You sent me a message reminding me my appointment today. We already had a meeting early yesterday. Is there an emergency situation? I'll be happy if you relieve my anxiety."

All of a sudden, Lucy's facial expression changed.

"Excuse me one second, please," she said and her image on the screen disappeared. When she came back, she posted the appointment records to Ben's screen. Then he saw that Ellie had an appointment with the doctor on the same day at the same time.

"Our records indicate sending you the message. Probably Dr. Anne wanted to see you and Ellie together."

"Are you sure?"

"It must be. I am reporting this to Dr. Anne."

Ellie and Dr. Anne's frozen images appeared on his screen again. He stood straight, took a deep breath and tried not to look stressed. He placed a fake smile on his face. A few seconds later, he took a seat across from Dr. Anne and attended the virtual meeting at the doctor's office.

Ellie sat next to Ben. She looked at him in surprise. She had an expression like Ben shouldn't have been there.

"Hi," said Ben, trying to figure out what was going on. When he said that he had knitted his eyebrows unintentionally.

"Hello," said the doctor. "Welcome, Ben."

"Hello," said Ellie. Her surprised expression had faded away. She sneaked a glance at Ben.

"Sorry, I couldn't reply to your request. I was connected a little early and the doctor accepted me when she was available. I had to refuse your request in order not to interrupt my meeting with her.

"I see," said Ben in a calm but cold manner. Though this hadn't made any sense for him. If they had started the meeting earlier, why hadn't Dr. Anne accepted his request?

"No problem. I just thought we could have a word on some issues, that's all," he added.

Then he remembered the doctor was there and turned to her.

"When I received two appointment messages on the same day, I thought there was an emergency situation and therefore I guess I interrupted your meeting. I should have waited for the meeting time."

"That's OK, Ben," said Anne. "There isn't an emergency situation. As far as I know there has been a miscommunication with Lucy about the appointment."

Ben first gave Ellie a short look. He thought he'd better stay there instead of later on wondering what they had talked about. Then he turned to Dr. Anne.

"I don't mind a second meeting."

After Ben's reply, she went into the subject in no time.

"I'd like to remind you of some important details so that you fully comprehend the process."

Although Ben was aware of Ellie giving him a look that made him feel as if he had done something wrong, he remained calm and focused on Dr. Anne.

"I had a meeting with both of you at the same time on your first appointment. The reason for that meeting was to canalize the use of your medical scanning activities in your PYXOMs to me and to keep you updated about the process you would be going through. But the next appointment had to be private. I believe you didn't read the file I sent to you completely before you approved it. In your files there is also information about your body rates and your reproduction hormone levels. The quality of the samples taken and their sufficiency information is also included in those files. This is considered private information. And it is not possible for us to share one adult's private information with another adult or with a third party. Therefore, our next meeting has to be private and separate. Since there has been a misunderstanding and both of you are here, let's have a general evaluation if you like. Later I'll speak with each one of you privately," she said.

"Sure," said Ellie and then turned and looked at Ben.

Ben nodded. He felt discouraged and so he wanted to keep quiet.

"Have you experienced any of the side effects that I told you about in our previous meeting?"

The grim expression on Ben's face changed slowly and relaxed. Could the medical treatment be the reason for his uncontrolled behaviors recently? But he couldn't tell the doctor what he was going through while Ellie was sitting next to him. He looked at Ellie hoping she would say something. She looked thoughtful and seemed she didn't want to say anything about it.

The doctor looked at them carefully and continued," OK, then let's skip the general evaluation and continue with our private meeting. Please, Ellie, you go ahead first."

"All right," said Ellie.

"I would like to talk to you privately if that's possible."

"Sure," said Dr. Anne and then turned to Ben, "I have to exclude you from this private meeting for a while, Ben. Lucy will take care of you."

Ben was wondering what Ellie would tell the doctor. He tried to make eye contact with her but he wasn't successful. The display on his screen froze, and in no time, Lucy appeared in front of him.

"Is there anything I can do for you, Ben?"

"No, thanks. I have a couple of calls to make, I'd like to take care of those while I'm waiting."

After Lucy disappeared from his screen, Ben stood up. He started moving along the hillside. He got close to the slope. There wasn't a way to know what Ellie and the doctor were talking about. He went back and sat on the rock he was sitting on before and started waiting, trying not to think or worry about anything.

After a while, a notification appeared on his screen saying that he would be included in the meeting and right after that he found himself in the doctor's virtual office, sitting next to Ellie.

Ellie welcomed him with a smile.

This means everything is OK. Did I worry over nothing? thought Ben.

"If you are ready, we can start the meeting now, Ben," said the doctor, interrupting his thoughts.

"Sure."

"Ellie, if you don't have anything else to tell me, we can end our meeting. As I said before, if you have a question, please free to contact me at any time. And please don't forget to take a look at the information I added to your file."

"Thank you, I will," said Ellie.

Ben was frowning again. There wasn't a reason for Ellie to wait, of course. Although she had a happy expression on her face, he couldn't figure out what she had in her mind. He hoped to have a private talk with her after the doctor's appointment, but he hadn't had a chance to tell this to her.

Ellie turned and smiled at him. Ben said "goodbye" and she left the meeting. He looked at Ellie's empty armchair for a while.

"Yes? I'm waiting for you, Ben."

Ben was startled with the doctor's voice. He stared at her.

"I'm sorry, what did you just say?"

"I asked for an additional approval from you for the evaluation of your body scan. I think you didn't hear me. Although I have authorization to use your PYXOM for medical purposes, you know I need your approval for every analysis.

"Oh, yes. Sure," he said, although he hadn't listened to the doctor after she said something about additional approval. He approved the doctor's request.

"I see that you have produced forty million sperm. Forty- two percent of them are active. Defect was found in thirty percent. A non-mutant normally needs to produce one hundred million sperms. I must say we have not reached the number of sperms by making a 0.005 change in your DNA for the baby you want. With the extra zinc and selenium support that I will add to your REST, I hope to achieve the necessary sperm level in 58 hours.

"When you said the baby you want... Do these levels stand for a baby boy or a baby girl?

"For a baby boy of course. As it is indicated in your file."

"Hasn't Ellie told you that she changed her mind?"

"No," said Anne.

"She wants a baby girl. I came to know this a few hours ago. I see that she hasn't informed you yet."

"The emotions she has been experiencing during this process must have fluctuated or even become extremely strong."

"What about you? As far as I understand you don't approve of her decision."

"I don't know. This happened so fast. Though I thought about it a lot, I couldn't come to a solution. I can't make any sense of Ellie changing her mind all of a sudden and not consulting with me about it. Since she told me this, my mind is so busy thinking that I didn't have time to decide if I want a baby girl or not. Besides, this decision change must be reported to the council. This means we have to wait for their reevaluation. While being a mentor is exciting and means a lot to me, I just can't adapt myself to this change."

After Ben stopped talking, the doctor waited for a while not saying anything.

"I see," she said finally, and added, "I think I should listen to Ellie as well in order to make this subject clear. Don't forget that the medications you are on will probably affect your reasoning ability. I can add a tranquilizer medicine to your REST that will calm you without affecting the clarity of your consciousness. Well, first of all I will need the approval from both of you before doing this."

At last Ben was relieved. He felt the emotional fluctuations inside him had eased a little after talking to the doctor about the subject.

"All right then, do you have anything else you would like to talk about?"

Ben straightened his back and sat straight. He hesitated for a few seconds, then, "Actually, I do."

"I'm listening,"

"The side effects you have mentioned… Isn't that normal?"

"It depends on the density of the side effects. What sort of distress?"

Ben stared at her for a while.

When she didn't receive an answer, she continued, "Let me remind you what we talked about in our recent meeting."

"Having emotional fluctuations is very likely. Besides this, you might have your sexual urges driving you or get unusually emotional. These are very normal and related to your testosterone levels. Did you experience anything different side effects than these?"

"No," he said without hesitation. "I have been experiencing similar things to what you have said for some time. I am having a hard time keeping my emotions under control and I began to think that this is affecting my life pretty much."

"Your worry is one of the side effects, but these are temporary and after you overcome this process, you will see them all disappear."

"You mean these are real?"

"We can't say unreal. Actually, the things you are experiencing are a part of human nature before mutation and at the same time these are the factors that prevent to reveal true human capability. As mutants you and Ellie are experiencing these emotions a lot more intensely than ordinary humans. Because in order to derive a proper chromosome matching, we have to produce three times more sperms and eggs than a normal human that hasn't been mutated. Also, even though it will be developed in artificial environment, to bring a child to our world, we have to raise these mutant hormones to above natural levels in the shortest period of time. This fast momentum is necessary for you to experience this difficult process in a shorter period. But from time-to-time this can put extreme pressure on you. After proper samples are collected and because your treatment will be over, you will change back to your mutant state slowly."

Ben was strangely saddened by what he had heard. And he didn't know how to handle this feeling. Did the doctor imply that all his feelings for Ellie would end? He had great admiration for her before the treatment, but his feelings were very different now. He was interested in her intelligence, her productiveness, and her contribution to humanity. Actually, this was respect and had nothing to do with gender. The reason for his desire to solve her was definitely on a logical basis. He wanted to know and understand a mastermind closely. During that period, he hadn't felt this desire as a dominating influence over him and he hadn't been disappointed either.

However, after the first part of the treatment, his desire had turned into an obsession he felt in all over his body and he wasn't able to control it. He had never wanted to touch a person or had ever felt his heart beating wildly for any reason until ten days ago. These things were new to him. Against all the negative effects these feelings had brought, deep inside there was something hindering him from escaping them.

"Then, I have a question," he said, finally having the courage to speak.

"I know that I have been deeply emotional lately, to my understanding, this is a part of human nature. Although these are so new to me and have a negative effect on controlling my life…"

He hesitated over continuing his speech for a while. Then he took a deep breath and thought he'd better continue if he wanted answers.

"Things I'm experiencing, how shall I put it… It's not easy to say but I think they are giving me a sort of pleasure that it's hard for me to define. To tell the truth, I'm kind of worried that these feelings will disappear when the treatment is over. I sense something that wasn't there before will leave a gap in my life when it goes away and this worries me."

"I understand," said Dr. Anne. "As I said before, all these are happening because of the treatment and when it's over you won't be feeling like this anymore. You had never felt this gap before as a human who had mutation. When your hormone levels turn back to normal, you won't feel it again. You'll be the person you were before. Even in your future life, when you remember these feelings, most probably they won't be making any sense to you."

Ben nodded, even though he wasn't satisfied with the doctor's answer. Maybe the best thing to do was to live and see. He had no other choices than this right now.

"During your REST session tomorrow night, you will receive the second part of the treatment. And during our next meeting we will collect samples to see if your testosterone levels are absolute as expected. Lucy will contact you for further details. Also, you might experience a noticeable amount of increase in the side effects right after the second treatment. If you would like to be informed about contingencies, you may find every detail in your file.

"Thank you," said Ben thoughtfully.

"Do you have any other questions?"

"Yes."

"You said the side effects would increase. But even now I am having a difficult time coping with them on this level. Today I tried so hard to ease my mind and I couldn't get any help from meditation either. For instance, I am having this meeting with you on top of a hill at The Grand Canyon. Even though I have been here for many minutes, this beautiful scenery wasn't enough for me to feel relaxed and comfortable. And also..."

When Ben realized that he was speaking impulsively, he hesitated. The doctor waited for him until he was ready to speak again.

"And also," he repeated, "I started to have feelings for Ellie, and I have no idea how to control these feelings."

He had finally confessed it to someone. This was so relieving for Ben and this had inspired him to speak more.

"This nuisance isn't in my brain only," he continued. "If you have noticed, my impatience causes me to act the way I never wanted to. I even misunderstood today's meeting time. After the unpleasant conversation I had with Ellie, I sent you a meeting request minutes before so that I could see and speak to her and when I couldn't get a reply from you I…"

He stopped. He shook his head as if he was trying to get rid of what he was about to say.

"I don't know myself anymore, Doctor. The changes in my mood reflect on my gestures and even on my tone of voice. Sooner or later others will notice this. For instance, when I think about my lesson today, I feel anxious. I am worried that I will ruin my dignity in front of my students."

"I think Ellie's decision change has intensified the side effects you have been experiencing so far. But this is not an unsolvable problem. I can add a tranquilizer to your REST session whenever you like."

Ben looked at her not knowing what to say and then, "I'd like to think about it. Is it OK if I inform you about my decision later?"

The doctor nodded.

"Thank you."

"Besides this, I advise you to keep your distance from Ellie as much as you can during this process. I believe this will be helpful. Meeting her very often will trigger the side effects. Well, it's up to you if you follow my advice or not. I will contact you about the child's gender after I meet with Ellie."

"Did you advise her to do the same? Is that why she is keeping her distance from me?" Ben asked abruptly.

As soon as he said this, he regretted how thoughtless he was. And taking his words back wasn't possible anymore.

First, the doctor frowned. Then her tensed up expression slowly turned into a relaxed one. She looked at Ben.

"Excuse me," he said as soon as he came to his senses. "I'm sorry."

"You already know that I can't talk about what I spoke with Ellie in private. And also, I advise you to consider taking the tranquilizer I mentioned earlier."

"Sure," he said in an embarrassed manner.

"Unless you have any other questions, we are done for today. You can contact me if you have further questions. I suggest you to examine your file."

"Well, of course. Thank you," said Ben and his connection ended.

He continued standing on the rock for a few minutes, not moving. He didn't know how to banish the things that had happened today from his mind. Ellie was quiet and looked happy before she left the meeting. He wondered if she felt the same and took pleasure in these feelings. Could she have feelings for Ben? If she had, then was she happy because the doctor had told her those feelings were temporary, or had the doctor really advised her to keep her distance from him and had this relieved her?

Maybe taking that tranquilizer would be a right thing to do since my questions are piling up like this, Ben thought.

Maybe it is something really good that will end the confusion in my mind soon, he said to himself. Then he got in to his vehicle and left there immediately at full speed.

Meanwhile, the KX3 observatory was still on highest level of alert. It was observing the movements of the black hole. There was a lump established in the middle of it. Soon, the expected happened; the black hole started to discharge energy. The observatory began to follow the process using blue Ner 3 rays.

Suddenly, an unidentified object popped out of the black hole at full speed. It traveled in the same direction as the white tube-shaped structure that came out of the black hole earlier. But this one was faster. It seemed like it tried to catch up with it. The unidentified object kept traveling at a speed of 18,775 miles per second.

CHAPTER 6

Ben had arrived one minute early. His class looked like a typical 21st century history class. He was teaching ten students between the ages of thirteen and eighteen. When he realized one of his students hadn't come yet, he leaned back and waited. This semester they had begun making travels in history. Students had to be bodily present in class in order to connect to HISD, a time leap device. When he saw the last student arriving, he saluted her with his head.

"Yes, my fellow friends," he addressed them. "I've observed that most of you were excited about our previous history travels in the last three classes. You directed to me many interesting questions after the recent class; I prefer to answer some of them here today. Especially, there were questions about Sumerians. You saw the time zone we wanted to explore had been dark and quiet during our travel. That is a period in history when humanity was stepping into a new age. There are many time zones that we can't observe. Your friend Zora had asked why we couldn't observe those periods."

Ben gave a pause and watched Zora and other students looking at him with curiosity, and then continued, gathering his palms on his chest.

"For instance, when I followed the person who wrote 22,000 tablets, I saw that his time period was dark as well. Actually, this is a very rare situation we come across in history travels."

"Professor, is it possible that it was darkened by a civilization that is more developed than ours?" Zora asked with a "know it all" expression on his face.

"Of course, we can't ignore this probability. But we don't know this for certain. Anyway, I believe in the future you will be able to solve this mystery that my generation isn't able to today."

"How come we can't research religions in our history classes?" asked Carla from the back. "Why is there a restriction although they emerged very long time ago?"

"This the Believers' area and they don't want us to intervene. And we respect their decision. If you want the answer, maybe you should direct this question to them."

After Ben finished his sentence, he waited for a while, then he made a gentle clap and said,

"No more questions today, OK, my friends?"

"Otherwise we won't have time for a travel. Shall we begin?" When he saw there weren't any objections, he continued.

"At this hour we will observe how Earth passed through and came out of the photon belt at the beginning of the 2000s and how this had affected Earth and humanity.

Ben paused for a while and made eye contact with each one of his students. He smiled when he saw the excitement on their faces, then continued.

"Earth passes through photon belt every 25,860 years. Our planet entered 'Null Zone' in the last phenomenon. This is the region where matter and particles of opposite matter collide to form proton parts of the belt. At the same time, it is the place where electromagnetic fields of Pleiades star system are nullified. For this reason, when earth passed through the photon belt, an energy form called electricity was no longer functional. At that time, it was an energy source for many vitally important mechanical devices and appliances that humanity had depended on. When it didn't function any more there was extreme devastation. We must understand thoroughly what our ancestors went through in that period. We will make a long travel to the depths of history."

He paused for a while so that the students would assimilate his speech. Moments later, when he saw them moving in their seats impatiently, he thought he had given them enough time. Then he took a deep breath while getting ready to speak. Students sat up straight in their seats and paid close attention to their history professor. He was pleased to have their concentration. He smiled and then continued with his speech.

"Don't forget that photon belt lasted a little more than two hundred years during the time the dinosaurs lived. When it began in 2070, it only lasted four years. Because at that time our planet did not completely go through photon belt and instead only came into contact with The Null Zone. There weren't severe effects to wipe out all life forms and humanity was able to pull through this dark period without extinction. Nevertheless, don't forget that it had a heavy impact on the population: fast and sudden drops occurred in a short period of time. Those were the times when people distorted the truth, and when a suitable part of reality was used to benefit one's self. They ignored the dark cloud on the horizon. And we will watch the consequences shortly. This much briefing is enough. Now, all of you lean back and authorize me access to your PYXOMs. After this, we may start visiting the time map I prepared for you. Besides, because the people of that period will be speaking a different language, don't forget to turn on the language translation mode."

Students made the necessary arrangements following their professor's directions. When Ben saw everyone had been connected, he issued a start command by winking his right eye. Their chairs stretched and transformed into recliners. Their PYXOMs on top of their heads got connected to an oval device that came out from the back of their recliners. The part above their necks got covered with a thin film.

"Soon you will feel the sense of falling into space. If you are all ready, I will count back from five and when I'm done counting, we will be starting our travel," Ben said and as soon as he saw they were ready, he started counting back.

First, they felt suction and then a strong pressure in their heads. Afterwards, the image of their history class began stretching, expanding, and then waving. Right after that they felt as if they were falling from a high cliff. Although this lasted only a few seconds, it was like minutes for the students. Then they found themselves in a pitch-black place; they felt like floating in the air. They could only move their heads and their bodies had turned numb. Shortly, they started hearing strange noises that sounded like fast rewinding voice records then a slow speech mode. They looked around uneasily but couldn't see anything but darkness.

"My fellows, we've completed the transition process! We are all there and everything is fine," they heard Ben's voice finally.

Then, they saw a shiny spot. First, they felt they were pulled by it slowly, and then they started moving in tremendous speed through a light tunnel. In a few seconds, they were thrown out of the tunnel into darkness at full speed. Then they slowed down and finally found themselves in outer space.

There was a mesmerizing view before their eyes. The earth that was about to pass through the photon belt stood right in front of them. From where they were, they could see both the sunny and the dark side of the earth. On the dark side, there were glitters of city lights. Soon, the dark side started moving toward the sunny side, wrapping it in a way to prevent sunlight reaching the Earth's surface. They watched the darkness spreading across the planet, and a few seconds later it was pitch black.

All of a sudden, their scenery changed. Now they were standing in the middle of a street, close to an intersection. Although it was daytime, it was twilight and the air was filled with grayish haze. They couldn't even read the signboards from where they were standing. In the distance, they thought the silhouettes of the buildings resembled Manhattan. They had seen the pictures of this borough many times before.

"A month later," they heard Ben saying, "Although humanity established many crisis management centers, those were never effective because the communication network had collapsed. And there had been disengagements from those groups. Therefore; everyone was alone in his or her life struggle. There wasn't a society that acted together or helped to heal each other's wounds. This caused a tragedy when people who sought for power started forming some sort of collaboration. As a result of this, a gang emerged in almost every neighborhood."

"Though their powers differed from zone to zone, the communities had to comply with this new order. There was chaos all over the world. Nobody was going out in the streets at nighttime. People tried to keep danger out by nailing plank wood on their windows, putting latches on their doors, and strengthening them with padlocks. People in shelters were luckier because they had suffered less from gang attacks. Under these circumstances, humanity was endangered. And consequently, in a short time, millions of people on Earth lost their lives. The president of the United States was one of the first persons among them. The secure room where the president was locked up with his presidential guards had been constructed with the highest technology of that time. This room was designed against manual entrance and when emergency power units and electricity were disabled, the president and his men were never able to get out. When rescue efforts did not turn out well and when hopes came to an end, disengagements occurred. Even the most loyal men of the president left him to death. Soon after, the White House was looted."

"It's important you understand the chaotic situation here well. People were aware that there wasn't much of a chance for them to survive. There was no ordinance of law or justice. Therefore, they thought they had to use all their energy and resources to support and protect their loved ones. There were prison breakouts. All weapons including nuclear weapons and ammunition remained unprotected. All grocery stores, hospitals, pharmacies and all sorts of stores were looted. And all this happened during the first three days of the photon belt. All armies and security forces were dispersed. All institutions, order, and finally all systems had collapsed. Against all efforts to protect sanctuaries, they were looted, too."

While the students were listening to Ben very carefully, they were watching this dark side of humanity with surprise and in terror. Then scenes from different streets started flowing one after another before their eyes. Streets had been closed with barrier blocks. There were armed men guarding each barrier; they were waiting, their hands-on triggers. Some men had machine guns and some had bazookas. All stores had been looted. Streets had been awash with blood; roads were covered with human corpses, dead animals, and litter. There were rats running around in every corner. Many wild animals had come to the city in order to find food. They saw boars, wolf packs and even a couple of bears.

"Day time on earth was a hazy twilight," said Ben.

"And night time was pitch black. The soil produced very few crops. All the food stocks and clean water springs were about to run out. People had to fight against hunger, deadly epidemics and especially freezing cold in winter. Besides this, they had to fight against looters and wild animals. Medicine production had stopped. In addition, many people were killing each other for a piece of food. Shortly, the population began to drop quickly."

Ben paused and took a deep breath. He gave them a few seconds to comprehend what they had seen.

"You have seen the general view," he continued, stressing each word.

"From now on, we will only observe without speaking unless it is necessary. I suppose, watching some sections of a particular family's life experience will better help you understand the traumas mankind had to live through during this period."

The scene blurred again and the students found themselves looking at a big room. The room had been lighted with a couple of candles and there were about twenty people; some were lying on cushions on the floor and some were sitting in the sofas next to each other, chatting. It was obvious they hadn't had a bath for a long time. The first thing that had caught their attention was their discouraged but careless looks. They covered their heads to protect them from the cold and their clothes were worn out. Their skins were pale, nails were broken, and their teeth were yellow.

They heard a rhythmic knocking on the steel door. At that moment, the people in the room silenced. Then one of the men pulled out his gun, walked toward the door, and looked through the peep hole. After that, he turned and told others that it was Mel. While everyone was relieved, the man quickly unlocked the door, pulled the latches and Mel, who was standing at the door with a dead eagle in his hand got inside. As soon as he got in, he found himself in a cube- shaped small cage made of steel plates. Then he slightly moved aside and waited for the door to close. He stood in the middle of the room saying nothing. Then he looked around while putting the bird on the ground slowly. A woman grabbed the eagle and examined it carefully. When she said it was edible, some of the people in the room started clapping their hands with joy; some were murmuring something their eyes closed.

A five or six-year-old girl got into the room.

"Dad is back!" she ran to the man who had brought the eagle.

"Yes, I am back, my sweet Emily," said Mel, picking up his daughter. "Where is your mom?"

"Over there," she said pointing at her mother.

"Pera is always sleeping, Dad," she said, frowning.

Mel looked where Emily was pointing; on the other side of the room was his wife. She was holding her baby and thoughtfully looking at the sky between the plank woods covering the window.

"Don't worry, sweetie, your brother will be just fine," he said. Then he kissed her on the cheek and put her down. He went near his wife.
"Do you think we will be able to see the stars and the moon again?" the woman asked, lifting her head, looking at Mel hopelessly.

"Of course, we will, Lisa," he said, faking a smile.

"There will be times you will be complaining about the heat. This pitch-black darkness will go away eventually," he added.

She tried to smile. "Yes, it will go away. It has to, right?"

Lisa noticed the medicine bottle Mel was holding. She looked at him again, not knowing what to say. Her eyes twinkled with joy.

Mel nodded while smiling. At that moment, the woman who had examined the eagle called out to him.

"Where did you get that antibiotic?" the woman said as she came near Mel. She grabbed the bottle from his hand and began examining it. "Nice," she said smiling

"There is more than enough of a dose here to make Pera well again. Wait here, I'll be right back with the right dose."

"Thank you, doc," said Mel, while the doctor walked away quickly.

Then he turned to his wife. He reached his son's forehead. The little boy was sleeping in her arms.

"How is he? Any changes?"

"His fever hasn't dropped. He's been sleeping for hours. He sometimes tosses in his sleep, that's all," she said, her voice trembling.

Mel waited for some time not pulling his hand away from Pera's forehead.

"There is diluted antibiotic here," the doctor said with a baby bottle in her hand. After shaking the bottle, she handed it to Lisa.

"Split it into six portions. You give it to him every six hours. His fever will drop. Don't worry, he will be fine," she said smiling.

"Just to let you know, I took some of it for later use," said Mel when the doctor walked away.

Lisa smiled at Mel. Then, after checking the measures on the bottle, she positioned Pera. She was able to give him the bottle while Pera struggled. When he finally started drinking it, Lisa took a deep breath instinctively. After giving him the required portion, she pulled the bottle gently from his mouth. She lifted her head and looked at Mel again. Then she touched the wound on his forehead after leaving the bottle in her hand.

"What happened?" she asked.

Mel pointed at the eagle that was being plucked on the other side of the room.

"Who found who?" asked Lisa smiling.

"I was walking home trying not to draw attention. You know, I was hiding in the corners. Suddenly I felt two claws gripping my shoulders. It was trying to lift me up. Out of the blue I lost my balance and my feet were dragged on the ground for a few seconds. When I looked up, I saw the eagle: it had a strange glitter in its eyes. It looked happy to find food and so was I. Then I quickly reached its neck and pulled it down with all my strength. And when it lost its balance, it couldn't take off. I reached my gun with my other hand, but while that it scratched my face with its beak. It's not a deep wound, just a scratch. Don't worry. Anyway, I have something else to tell you; I have good news," he said smiling.

She looked at him with curiosity.

"The people camping at the Lincoln tunnel happened to be my friends from the university. They helped me cross to New Jersey today," said Mel excitedly.

Lisa's face brightened up. "Really?" she asked. But still she doubted.

"Yes, we can start our journey from there."

Lisa stood up after carefully placing the baby in an armchair. She hopped a couple of times clapping with joy. Then she stopped and looked around anxiously.

"But when are we going to tell them?" she asked referring to the people in the room with them.

"We can tell them after dinner," said Mel. "No need to wait."

Suddenly, the scene before their eyes began blurring and waving. Right after that, the scene of the same room appeared. This time everyone was sitting and no one was speaking.

Mel and Lisa were next to each other. Pera was in his mother's arms; Emily was sleeping on one of the cushions on the floor. Mel straightened his back, moved forward slightly in his seat and then looked at Lisa. She showed her acceptance by smiling at him, and so he took a deep breath.

"My friends I have something important to tell you," he said finally. Then he waited for a while and when he was sure that he had everybody's attention, he continued.

"We have decided to leave the city and we are planning to leave after five days."

At first, everyone looked at one another in surprise. Then murmuring got louder; they asked why they would leave and where they would go.

"I think everybody in this room agrees assuming that Earth is passing through the photon belt," then he continued. "And we don't know how long this darkness will last. Who knows, maybe we will end up like dinosaurs? Still, we have hope. But we think staying in the city will lower our chances to survive. There are epidemics everywhere, we have difficulty breathing, and things are getting worse everyday."

"Listen! You hear that?" he said after they heard the gunshots coming from outside.

"Look, every day the clashes between the armed gangs are becoming more violent."

"We have guns, too!" a young man shouted.

"How do you know other places are different from here?" said another man.

Mel raised his arm and silenced the men.

"OK, you're right. There is trouble everywhere, but again we believe circumstances would be different out there. That's why we are leaving and we want you to join us."

"Under these circumstances, it is very difficult for us to survive in the wild," said their doctor friend. Especially when every living being has gone mad in this cold and darkness …"

"Most of us have never really fought against the harsh conditions of nature. We are not country men. We don't know how to deal with soil or herds. How is that going to happen?" said another person.

"We can't survive. Even the streets of the city are filled with wolves. They can't even live in their habitat. How in the world is it possible for us to survive when they can't? We would be bait for wild animals. At least we are here together in collaboration and we are powerful as long as we stay together," said the woman sitting across Mel.

"Don't we try to survive here in this wild and violent city?" asked Mel.

"You're right. But against all the violence, we have a house that protects us from the cold and dangers of outside," replied the doctor.

"What about the water problem? We don't know how long this situation will last. After some time, most probably the biggest energy and oxygen resource will be water. And each day, it is getting harder to reach clean water supplies. Soon there will be a problem with oxygen. How are we going to fight against epidemics?"

"We can overcome those issues here," said the doctor.

"I wish I could agree with you. I wish all of you were right. My reasoning is that we should leave before it's too late," said Mel.

Everyone was silent; they were deep in thought.

"Lisa and I made a plan. We can stock necessary food and items, cross to New Jersey and from there we can move on to safer places."

"How can you be so sure that you can get there?" asked a middle-aged man. "Every corner is controlled by gangs."

Mel took a map out of his pocket and laid it on the coffee table in front of him.

"We will follow this path till we get to the Lincoln tunnel," he said, pointing to the path he had marked on the map. "The people controlling the tunnel are my friends. I marked all the open and closed roads on the map, there... And this is the path we will follow after we pass through the tunnel."

"This is an unreliable plan, Mel," said a woman. "We can't take the chance, since there are so many unknowns. This house is safer compared to the outside. We know where we are and our conditions. Therefore, it's insane to go on a journey full of danger."

A loud humming noise filled the room; everyone agreed with what she had said. Nobody in the room was open to that leaving plan.

"You should also stay here," said the doctor, turning to Lisa, her eyes pleading.

Then she added, "Pera hasn't recovered yet. We have a chance to find medicine here, but if you leave and one of you gets sick, how will you provide medicine? We have collaboration here, right? We are looking after another. We are safer here."

Lisa held her hand in her palms and said softly, "Don't worry, we will be fine. Pera will recover because of you, and I am grateful for this. But staying here is riskier for him, too. The epidemic threat will go away to a great extent when we leave the downtown. He is so little and there are diseases all around. And water shortage is around the corner. We think it's irrational to stay. And we believe our chance to survive out there is better than staying here."

"We have five more days," said Mel. "You all think about what we said. We'll discuss this again later." Then he looked at his golden-chained pocket watch around his neck that he had inherited from his grandfather.

"I don't want to miss the daytime tomorrow," he said standing up. "If you excuse me, I want to sleep."

The flabbergasted students had been observing the scenes quietly when the view on their screens blackened.

"Because we have limited time, we are visiting only the family's most critical moments and how they lived through those times. If you would like to follow these closely, please let me know," said Ben while the scenery changed on the students' screens.

This time they saw a structure surrounded by walls like a fort. Under the wall, there was a family trying to enter. Lisa was holding her baby and she looked exhausted. Emily was holding her dad's hand, shivering from cold. Behind them was a wagon with a long handle loaded with items.

Mel let go of Emily's hand, took a few steps and looked up.

"Please accept us!" he shouted over the wall.

There was no answer.

"Let us in! Please!"

No answer again. They could hear the running feet in the silence of the night. It was getting late and it was dark. Outside was cold but there were 6.5-foot torches burning with flames. They were arranged with spaces between by the walls.

"Thank God they lit these," said Lisa, her voice trembling. She took Emily's hand and walked toward the torches to get warm.

"If there weren't these torches, we might have passed by the colony without seeing it."

"I don't think they lit them for attraction," said Mel turning to Lisa. "They have no intention of letting us in."

"So, they don't want company." Then she hesitated and looked around.

"Maybe there are many animal attacks in this area. Look at the size of these torches."

"Maybe, but I don't think these torches will help to keep the animals away; there is pretty much space between them. Probably they lit them to protect themselves from the epidemics; to kill the germs at least," said Mel and looked up again but there was no one.

Then they heard a growling. Later, the noise came nearer.

"Darn it! Come here, quick, by the wall!" said Mel in a hurry while running to his wife and kids.

"Shoot! It must be the wound on my arm; they must have gotten the smell of my blood. Come on, stand closer to the wall."

When Lisa hid Emily behind her and got her back to the wall, she looked around anxiously.

Mel ran to the wagon and took a can. Then he shook it to check how much gas was left in it. He didn't have time to get near the big torches.

"We have to use the rest of the gas. I hope this will be our last challenge," he said.

Then he positioned himself on Lisa's left and took a couple of steps forward; starting from the wall, he drew a circle by pouring the gas. Then he took a lighter out of his pocket and fired it up. While taking a few steps back, he pulled his gun from his waist, and checked the magazine. He only had two bullets left.

"Only two left out of almost two thousand bullets," he said while reaching the wagon. He grabbed the rifle and the axe next to the rope and pulley and placed them on the ground. He turned, picked up Emily who had been wrapped around her mother's leg with fear. He placed her in the wagon and Lisa laid the baby down next to her sister carefully.

"Don't be afraid sweetie, everything will be fine," she said while patting Emily's hair kindly.

"No lifting the blanket before I say so. OK?"

When Emily nodded, Lisa smiled at her.

"You will be safe and sound here, don't worry sweetie," she said and covered them with the blanket.

Then she picked up the rifle from the ground.

"How many have you got?" asked Mel while picking up the axe from the ground.

"Two,"

"So, we have four altogether. Better than nothing," he said smiling. Then he stared at the darkness behind the fire, waiting quietly.

Soon they saw the wolves. They were moving closer, passing slowly the spaces between the torches.

In a few seconds, five big wolves had surrounded the flames right in front of them; they were moving forward, here and there, looking for a spot where they could pass over.

"This is not good," said Mel. "But we can make it. If we can identify the alpha and kill it, the pack might go away after that"

Then they heard whisperings from above. Following that, keeping an eye on the wolves, Mel shouted one more time hoping to get an answer.

"Please let us in. We don't want food."

"What's that around your neck? Is that a pocket watch with a chain?" asked a man's voice.

"We won't be a burden, we only need a place to spend the night. We don't want food."

"Does that watch work?" asked another man.

"Yes, it's in real good condition."

"Toss it up!"

"First open the door, then you can have the watch."

"Suit yourself. We can take it after the wolves have eaten you," said the man.

"You're not in a position to bargain," said another man.

Mel said nothing looking up for some time.

"Come on, can't you toss it up fifteen feet?"

"What if you can't catch it and it breaks?" asked Mel. "Then it's no good to you. Let us in and the watch will be fine."

"If you make a good throw, we'll catch it, of course. But if you can't and it breaks, you'll lose your chance to get in."

What if I toss it into the fire, who will benefit from this?" asked Mel, while reaching out to the fire holding the watch. "What if you don't let us in after I give it to you?"

Then a woman's voice was heard behind the wall. "Enough, Mark!" she screamed. "Stop this stupid bargain. They have small kids. Don't you see that?"

"Yes, stop it!" said other women all together.

"Show mercy!" screamed another woman.

"Hold it, you're letting them in now, that's the end of this conversation."

In a second there was silence. Mel watched the wolves around the fire while waiting for an answer from the people behind the wall. Flames were high, there was still time. Finally, he instinctively put the axe on the ground, took off the chain around his neck, and tossed it up in an instant. At that moment, he saw many hands reaching for the watch, trying to catch it. Then, one of them grabbed it.

"Where did you get this?" asked someone.

"It was my grandfather's. Because I can't see behind the flames well, I can't tell which one is alpha. Can you tell?" Mel shouted.

"Has it been working since the power was out?"

"Yes," said Mel, keeping an eye on the wolves. "I wound it every day since then. Tell me which one the alpha is?"

"Do you know how much time passed since the power was out?"

"Yes," said Mel, then reached to the wagon and took out two books.

"Look! I have books, too. This tells you how to survive in the wild," he said raising one of them, and then he raised the other book.

"And this is about root plants and vegetables," he added.

"You would be shocked if you knew how many edible root plant and vegetables there are. I know them all very well and the healing herbs, too. I have so many things that would be useful to you, and even a fishing rod."

"What's your name?" said an authoritarian voice that he had not heard before.

"Mel, and this is my wife Lisa."

"We have two kids in the wagon," said Lisa while lifting the blanket.

"Emily and Pera. Our son isn't even two yet. Please let us in."

"You might be carrying a disease. You will stay in quarantine for a while," said the same voice.

"Thank you. We are grateful sir," said Mel, realizing the man was the colony leader.

"But I can't promise for tomorrow. We make decisions here by vote. We will see if you are staying or leaving tomorrow morning. And also, you will hand over all your weapons when entering our lodge."

"OK," said Mel with excitement.

Then Mel and Lisa looked at one another smiling.

"From left to right, pick a target!" the man shouted.

"Don't waste bullets, aim at the head. I don't want to lose another tooth while I'm eating. Ready! And…Fire!"

They heard the shots fired. Each wolf was killed with one shot on the head.

"Open the door. Don't make our guests wait," said the leader.

"The huge wooden door opened with a loud squeal. Mel, Lisa and their kids entered slowly. Despite their exhausted appearance, both of them had gleams of hope in their eyes.

"Yes, my fellows," they heard Ben saying, while the view was fading away.

"I hope you understand well the difficult times this family had to experience. Don't forget, they were the lucky ones despite all the challenges they had to face. Many tragedies had been lived through during those four years on the Earth. The reason I chose this family for your observation is, they were the few that had to make difficult choices. They had foreseen the unexpected and had been able to survive. They are the ones and people like them; our ancestors who continued our generation," he said and paused, giving the students some time to think about the scenes they had watched.

"Ellie's great-great-grandparents," he said to himself. He had started observing this family because of his desire to explore her past relatives. He even had watched the scenes he hadn't shown to his students. He had watched them may be ten times. He thought he would know Ellie better by knowing them. But he couldn't have told this to his students. On the other hand, he was honest about why he had chosen this family for his history lesson. Although his reason to pick that family was Ellie, as he observed them more, he had explored their importance in history and had started admiring them for this. There couldn't have been a better example for his lesson.

"Let me go over the scenes that you did not watch," said Ben and then continued.

"His friends who stayed in the city and didn't want to take risks couldn't survive for long time. Because they couldn't foresee how they would suffer from lack of water and food. And because of the increase in violation, murder and epidemics they couldn't make an attempt to leave their house that they thought was safe. There were so many other reasons that triggered their termination. First of all, there weren't many trees in the city. During day time there wasn't enough sunlight for trees to produce oxygen through photosynthesis. In a short time, besides thirst and hunger, they had to breath the air that had a very low oxygen level."

"The night before Mel and Lisa left the house, they had slept hugging their guns. Their fingers were on the trigger while gunshots were fired, wolves and half-breed wild dogs howled on the streets outside. The next morning, they loaded their wagon, said goodbye to their friends and left the city. They passed deserted towns and came across with thousands of skeletons of people slaughtered and eaten by wild animals. They moved on their path collecting things they thought might be useful and so their load became very heavy in time."

"Nights were the toughest. They had to find a place to sleep. Their sleeping place was sometimes an abandoned house, a factory building, a barbershop, or even a grocery store. This changed almost every night. Mel had sleepless nights so that his wife and children could sleep in safety. Some nights he had to struggle with wild dogs, wolves, and once with a bear. They passed many colonies but none of them accepted Mel and his family. They were miserable and exhausted and it had taken them six weeks to arrive at this previous colony. If they were rejected again, their survival would have been in peril."

Ben paused again and took a deep breath. "That's all for the summary," he said.

"After four years of darkness, the photon belt period came to an end and the Earth had its sunlight again. Now, let's continue analyzing what the family we've observed went through this period."

After Ben completed his sentence, students found themselves in a completely different scene. It was spring and nature had been revived by sunlight. People's skin was glowing. Grizzly soil had turned into green grass. Pera had grown. He and the children were running to the boat where his sister was. Emily, with a plastic bucket in her hand, jumped out of the boat as soon as it reached the shore. Pera and children looked inside the bucket with excitement. It was filled with a lot of fish.

"Can I carry it?" asked Pera looking at Emily with begging eyes.

"Sure," said Emily. Pera grabbed the bucket and then started running happily with his friends.

"Slow down!" Emily called after them.

Then the view blackened again. A big round table with people crowded around it appeared in front of them. One of them was Mel. He was sitting at the table.

"Two years later Mel and his family were accepted by the colony, he was chosen as a new leader when Mark died of a disease," said Ben.

"Our world needs a new order; a peaceful order without any sort of weapons. We are here today because we share the same idea. This meeting is the first step for uniting people from all over the world. Our top priority must be to ensure a peaceful setting. Therefore, we should focus all our efforts on this matter." Then Mel continued after a short pause.

"It is an advantage to have friends of military origin among us. We will need their knowledge and skills. All firearms and deadly weapons must be taken under control. We must move the ones who got used to performing violence and unjust use of force to an isolated area and neutralize them. By this, they will be able to establish the order they want kept away from us. We must not let them profit from the civilization we will establish. They must provide their own accommodation and food. As long as they keep their distance from our new order..." Ben turned off the sound in the scene and gave an explanation.

"This speech lasts almost half an hour. The people around the table are the leaders of other colonies. They are discussing the precautions they could take against any threat from outside their colonies. In a short time, this association assembly will expand with the participation of other colonies."

All of a sudden, students found themselves getting a bird's eye view of Egyptian Pyramids shining under the sun in the middle of a desert. They saw a big tent right next to the pyramids. Then the view blurred and after a moment of blackening, they started watching the scene in the big tent. There were hundreds of people from different races in it. There were children playing around, some women holding babies and some were chattering feverishly. Time to time, there were laughter heard among the loud crowd.

In the tent, Mel was standing on a platform. A thirteen or fourteen-year-old girl was sitting in Mel's armchair. Her back was straight and she had crossed her legs. She was smiling to her friend across for a photo shoot. This was Emily, Ellie's great-great-grandmother. Another mystery was solved. At his previous meeting with Ellie, she was sitting exactly in the same position. Somehow, she probably had found the picture her friend had taken, thought Ben.

"When the last tree is cut down, the last fish eaten, and the last stream poisoned, you will realize that you can not eat money," Mel started his speech.

Suddenly there was silence in the tent; kids went to sit next to their parents and everyone paid attention to Mel.

"When the last tree is cut down, the last fish eaten, and the last stream poisoned, you will realize that you can not eat money," he repeated after a short break.

"We were able to adopt this vintage Indian saying and its value centuries later. All of you are welcomed to the grand assembly! Five years passed since the first sunny day after twenty-seventy. Today is the day for all universes to celebrate. Today is the day when humankind was reborn. Today is the day when borders disappeared, money did not exist, and the first day of the constitution that all humankind agreed upon!"

"Three words…Yes, we are here today for these three: Universe, Harmony, Life. These three words gathered us here. To add new meanings and values to these concepts will be our and the next generations' major duty. We don't perceive this mission awareness as law-abiding. Because laws are impositions for people that don't have the ability to bless, to respect, or to conform to the peerless existence in the universe. But we should leave these behind us and must confront the difficulties on this path decisively. Because we know that every step on this path will take humankind to the happy home of the next generation. From now on every new-born is our planet's child."

"We will build a common language, we will both learn and teach mankind's new language to our children. Every person will be free to live the way they like as long as they are respectful to the values of "Universe, Harmony, and Life". We will not produce anything that is not in harmony with nature. Right, wrong, deficiencies…we will debate these issues in our committees. We will share all with our society. We will receive their approval. If necessary, any kind of weapon that will cause violence, against all armed gangs-"

The view before Ben and his students suddenly disappeared. They felt a great pressure in their heads and a brown light started flashing on the screens of their PYXOMs.

BROWN ALERT
BROWN ALERT
High risk of danger alarm code

SOURCE:
The scanner satellite positioned on Earth's Stratosphere layer

MISSION DEFINITION:
To ensure the continuity of life safety on Earth. To scan the atmosphere in order to detect any danger coming from outer space in advance, to define possible sources and terminate them.

REASON FOR ALERT
Alien virus, unidentified entity

Ben discontinued the lesson after he was sure all the students came back smoothly.

CHAPTER 7

Ellie was at home getting ready for the meeting with The Paradox Brain committee when a conversation request popped up on her screen. This was Lucy, Dr. Anne's assistant.

She didn't have a chance to review the folder the doctor had forwarded a couple of hours ago. She wondered if there was something important. Although she had five minutes to her conference with the committee, she was dying of curiosity so she accepted the request.

"Hello, Ellie," said Lucy.

"Hello."

"If you are available, Dr. wants to have a short meeting with you."

"Actually, I have three minutes only."

Lucy waited for Ellie's answer.

"All right," said Ellie

"I am connecting you to the virtual meeting. Please confirm."

"Thank you."

As soon as Lucy's image disappeared, a meeting request appeared and as she confirmed it, she found herself in the doctor's office.

Anne welcomed her with a smile.

"Hello," said Ellie, while taking her seat across from the doctor, trying to hide her uneasiness.

"Hello, Ellie. I wanted to talk to you in reference to the information I received from Ben during my meeting with him. I'm not going to take much of your time."

While one of her eyebrows lifted, Ellie moved her head sidewise slightly.

"It's about the gender of your future baby," said Anne, satisfying Ellie's curiosity.

"Oh, yes," said Ellie and turned her eye away. "So, Ben told you."

"Yes, this is important. We need to make it clear. We will change the treatment according to your decision."

"I see," said Ellie after she hesitated.

"I was going to let you know after Ben and I had an agreement," she added.

"So, do you have an agreement then?"

"No, not yet."

"Then I would like to give you a third option."

"What is the third option?" she asked with curiosity.

"First of all, I would like you to know that there is a significant vacancy in our population quota that is expected to be filled. Therefore, every application is very valuable for humanity. But we have to discontinue your treatment until you make your final decision and this is not a situation we really prefer."

Ellie sighed. Ann waited for a while thinking she would say something.

"Actually," she said when she discovered Ellie was not going to respond, "This might have a negative effect on you. The reason we don't prefer is not only the quota; our priority is your well-being. You have already been affected by this treatment; we increased your hormone levels and this is a burden to you both physically and psychologically. Therefore, taking a long break in your treatment means starting this process from the very beginning and this burden will be heavier than before."

"I see," said Ellie in a thoughtful manner. "OK...You just mentioned a third option. What is that?"

"Twins."

"Twins?" asked Ellie, her eyes wide open although her voice was calm.

"Yes, by this way you can have them both, a girl and a boy. And you won't have to make a choice in between."

Doctor Anne became silent and gave her some time to think while Ellie was still and staring at a point on the wall.

"Does this require a major change in our treatment?" she asked finally turning to the doctor.

"At this point, there won't be more of a burden than changing the gender of a baby. The most important factor is not having a long-time interruption in your treatment. I advise you to have a session in the next forty-eight hours. By this way your hormone levels wouldn't be dropping and we won't be extending the process of your treatment needlessly. Well, if there will be twins, there will be an increase in the number of samples we will be collecting. This only means a little increase in dose. It's definitely not an easy decision. It will be helpful to notify us of your decision in forty-eight hours for the internal system planning," said Doctor Anne.

"All right, I'll think about it. I will evaluate this with Ben and we will notify you before forty-eight hours."

"I'd like to remind you that the sooner you make a decision, the less your treatment dose will increase."

"Sure, I understand."

"Have you thought about receiving tranquilizers?"

"I didn't have time to think about it. I have very limited time; I have to be in a conference in a hundred seconds. I will notify you about that as soon as possible."

"All right then, Ellie, I am looking forward to hearing from you."

"Thank you and have a nice day," said Ellie smiling and ended the meeting.

"What time is it?" she asked right after that.

"14:28:25" said the voice in the apartment.

She had very little time but she wanted to take a short look at her notes.

"Conference notes," she said to her PYXOM. "Accelerated presentation," she added.

While the images were flowing fast on her screen, in order to give a final check, she started to look over the notes.

It had been ten seconds only since her final check when all of a sudden, the screen froze and brown lights started to flash on her PYXOM's screen.

BROWN ALERT
BROWN ALERT
High risk of danger alarm code

SOURCE:
The scanner satellite positioned on Earth's Stratosphere layer

MISSION DEFINITION:
To ensure the continuity of life safety on Earth. To scan the atmosphere in order to detect

any danger coming from outer space in advance, to define possible sources and terminate them.

REASON FOR ALERT
Alien virus, unidentified entity

COORDINATES
(^^) HC7ZZ0014A

A globe that symbolized Earth appeared on PYXOM's light screen. It was surrounded with a green ring inside and a blue ring outside. The globe got bigger until it zoomed on Prescott; a city in old America's Arizona state.

DISTANCE
1 mile 12 feet

DIRECTIVE
PYXOM must be sent

TRACK DATA
1st degree importance

Ellie was looking at her screen in surprise. Then she gathered herself up and ordered her second PYXOM to go to the scene. She had forgotten all about the conference.

"How can this be possible?" she murmured while moving from left to right on her KRYXO in the room. She couldn't figure out where the virus could have come from. It couldn't have been emitted from the Believers' land; this was impossible. The whole region was covered with an isolation screen that held all the living organisms inside. It wasn't possible for Believers to leave their land before entering the quarantine to get disinfected.

"Then where could have this virus come from?" she wondered. She stopped moving around in the room.

"It came out of nowhere but from where?"

The scene was very close. Ellie enlarged the map quickly. The source of the virus was one mile north east of HB7 commune that they lived in. She could observe the scene from the five hundredth floor of the building.

"500th floor scenery," she commanded her PYXOM in order to find out what was going on.

In a moment her body was floating in the air. This was the top floor of the colony building where most of the commune members of the world lived. She zoomed in on the target 300 times. She detected a small area covered with brown smoke. While she was watching, the color of the smoke turned to red first then to orange and finally to yellow. Afterward the air was clear, the smoke had gone completely, and there appeared a naked hairy man.

She tried to make sense of this, but she couldn't. She had no idea what was happening. So, this gave her an urge to have a closer look of the scene from a different perspective. She was witnessing a very creepy incident and although she could see this with her own eyes, her mind doubted.

Could this be a game played by the Believers? she thought.

Her knowledge and experience could not explain this. She needed more data to understand what this was, but her second PYXOM hadn't arrived at the scene yet.

Eventually, she changed her vision back to normal by removing the zoom in her eye and got back to the level of her apartment floor. She requested the recording of the incident from the satellite right away. After all, she was one of the few scientists who had a right for access to the satellites at large.

She began analyzing the incoming data in no time. The brown alert code had been given for a small area exactly thirty seconds ago. The virus had appeared from out of nowhere and its origin hadn't been detected.

She couldn't believe her eyes while she was watching this; a mass of white cloud flowed out of a one-millimeter diameter hole with high pressure. Then, the cloud turned into a balloon as soon as it came in contact with air and colorful gases inside were activated forming the shape of a human being. After that, the image inside the balloon became more visible. It turned white and then cracked open and finally let the creature out as if it was giving birth. In less than a second, the balloon turned into a cloud. It shrank back to one millimeter in diameter and disappeared at the spot where it came from. At that moment, the virus had been detected. Following that in order to eliminate the virus, it was surrounded with a brown fog. The color of the cloud turned red, then orange, and then finally to yellow. Right after this, the colorful fog disappeared completely. The virus had been wiped out in fifteen seconds.

While Ellie was trying to explain what she had seen, her PYXOM arrived at the scene and started sending live images from a 360-degree angle. She observed the new data with great excitement.

The visitor looked like a male human being. He was naked and also had body hair. He had long black hair divided in the middle. He was looking around puzzled, covering his genitals with both hands. Ellie's expression wasn't different from his while watching him. Her eyes were wide open, as she hadn't seen anything like this before. She was looking at the screen paying close attention, trying to figure out what was happening.

With that, the region was filled with PYXOMs. Because they were made of super lenses supported by gamma local vibration and could bend light, they couldn't be seen with the naked eye. Their number had risen to thousands in a short time. It was possible that the number could go up to tens of thousands in minutes. All humanity had concentrated on this incident; they had begun watching it as soon as the images were transferred. The visitor, not knowing or seeing those devices or the building that was equipped with high technology, was just looking around while thousands of eyes watched him.

The stranger didn't look threatening, on the contrary he looked so desperate that Ellie noticed that she pitied him for a second. Then, surprised by her behavior, her reasoning took over and she tried to evaluate the incident on a rational basis.

However, her reasoning wasn't helping her much either. Although this unknown stranger had created uneasiness, her mind could not detect any kind of danger in his looks, gestures, or in his body language. When Ellie analyzed him more carefully, she realized there was a mature and solemn expression on his face despite his young age. His green eagle eyes had brightened his skinny, dark-colored features.

His body language implied his uneasiness. He seemed like he didn't know Earth or its science or technologies. Even though he couldn't see them, he would know the PYXOMs were around him. He would try to communicate with people through them and would ask for help by telling people about the reason for his fear and confusion. Instead, he was looking around as if he was unaware of any of these. And he looked really desperate.

PYXOMs had shortly measured his brain waves, taken his pulse, and analyzed his gestures in order to make analysis of his personality. As a result, they had defined him as "Peaceful". Ellie turned out to be right with her assumption.

Ellie was somewhat relieved, but although there wasn't any data that proved he would show some sort of aggression, it was still too early to start a communication with him. Yet, the stranger's dominant emotion was detected as "Fear" and this emotion was very hard to control for someone who hadn't been mutated. This situation could have turned him into an aggressive being. Therefore, they needed more information about this stranger before contacting him.

Then, Ellie saw a message from the Council. They had started voting because the unrestrained increase of PYXOMs at the scene could have enhanced the probability of inaccuracy. She cast her vote right away. In seconds, the voting was completed by participation of thousands. Later the suggestions were evaluated. As a result of the voting, it was decided that common use PYXOMs were to be positioned by the system at the scene. Although there was no obligation to follow, everyone, including the voters voted against the idea, pulled back their PYXOMs from the scene. Only specialists' devices were given the permission to move freely beside the common use PYXOMs. These devices were still watching this man-like creature from every angle.

The images PYXOMs captured had reached to all people in the universe. Analysis was coming steadily. There was fast data flow about the eliminated virus but the scientists could not reach a conclusion about how and where this had come from. The first findings indicated a flu virus. It had similarities with the first influenza virus recorded in 1510 but it wasn't an exact match.

This virus had caused more than twenty-five million to die in 1918. The areas and dates of this epidemic were reflected on the PYXOM screens graphically. But all this information was not sufficient for Ellie or other scientists. There were many questions waiting for answers. How had this virus breached all that scanning? The tracks said it had neither come from space or underground. This virus was not active on Earth for six hundred years and that meant it definitely had to come from somewhere else.

Also, the stranger had body hair. Except for the Believers, it had been 160 years since people had given up on all the hair on their bodies. This stranger couldn't be one of the Believers because they would never leave their territory before going through quarantine. The reason for living in peace for hundreds of years despite all their differences was each society respecting other society and their rules without exception.

No, Ellie thought. This being must have come from somewhere else but where? And most importantly, how?

In the meantime, they had located a piece of hair. It was analyzed right away and its genetic map was presented; 30,000 genes and around

100,00 proteins that were encoded by these genes. He was definitely a human being. The system had scanned the DNA base but had no match with any of the people living on Earth. This meant that the visitor had no relation with anyone on Earth today.

Investigation commissions from all around the universe had already been established by academicians of different fields interacting with one another. New developments were monitored, evaluated, and disputed. These academicians were trying to form theories so that they could find answers to the questions where he came from and who he was. The everyday life on Earth had almost come to a stop with the brown alert. Everyone was watching the stranger and following the debates in the commissions at the same time.

Meanwhile, the visitor's body scans started and his gene map was presented; no anomalies were found in his body or organs. He was very young, almost eighteen. His brain wasn't developed much but he was sending out a frex that they hadn't encountered before. Findings of his stomach were interesting; there were lamb meat, grapes, date and wheat remainders. His genetic was not interfered; he was an undeveloped human being.

The probable diseases he might face in future and hundreds of findings were being shared with all people using their PYXOMs.

At last the Council made a statement. Commissions had made their first report; this man-like stranger was a young male; his name was not identified and therefore this stranger was given a name called "ZA".

Ellie decided to analyze his DNA one more time hoping to find a hint. But she was not able to focus because she couldn't take her eyes away from the images her PYXOM had been sending. She couldn't help looking at his body and the genitals ZA was trying to cover. He remembered Gabe while they were kids playing and when they had touched each other's genitals secretly. She was excited. Thinking of Gabe was enough to make her heart beat faster, just like in those days.

What's wrong with me? she thought and felt uneasy. Despite her mutation, all she was experiencing was bothering her. Side effects of her treatment were pretty heavy even in a state of brown alert. She was having trouble concentrating on work and this was unusual.

I should accept the tranquilizer treatment, she thought.

Yes, this would be a right thing to do. She felt a little relief with her decision. Then she forced herself to pay attention to the images of ZA sent from her PYXOM.

The stranger had entered the grove. He broke an ivy branch and immediately afterward he picked two leaves from a fig tree.

Ellie and everyone that were watching the stranger's actions froze.

The data on the screen had changed rapidly. His description had changed from "Peaceful" to "Aggressive".

The Council sent another message. It was advised no one to contact this "Aggressive" being no matter what his/her access level was.

All humanity was terrified as they had never felt or seen anything like this before. Ellie was also very annoyed with what she had seen. How dare a stranger interfere in this ecologic system? Believers and other colonies were free in their relation with nature in their own environment. But in this region an action like this was considered as aggressiveness and was not tolerated. This stranger could not have belonged to Earth. This was an extra-ordinary situation. Ellie was mad at herself for pitying him before. She was very disappointed for analyzing this stranger wrong. Besides, she wasn't the only one, PYXOMs had wrong analysis as well.

The silence of humanity was finally broken. The statements of many specialists like eco scientists, natural living coordinators, nutrition controllers and ecological balance conservators were broadcast one after another. The damage caused by breaking the branch of that ivy and picking two fig leaves was enormous because these actions were untimely, out of control, and unmeasured. There was a huge distortion of ecological balance. All calculations had to be made all over again and a new program had to be developed for recovery. The water loss in the ivy and the fig tree and its effect to other branches couldn't be underestimated. It was obvious that the stranger who performed such action was totally irresponsible. No matter what, his further actions similar to the previous one had to be prevented.

The Council stepped in. Suggestions were gathered. All specialists deepened their analysis in their fields. The stranger was put under a microscope.

In the meantime, ZA was looking around uneasily, unaware of the hustle around him. Right after that he began peeing under the fig tree that he had picked the leaves from.

Humanity hadn't got over the first incident yet and they were terrified with this one for the second time.

With that, the Council had made a decision after evaluating the suggestions. The tree and the area surrounded it were put to rehabilitation in an invisible shield so that the damage would be repaired and the area wouldn't be exposed to any further damage.

A message popped up on Ellie's screen. This was Ben. In his message, he was saying that he had permission from the Council to investigate and record the time of ZA's appearance by making a time travel to that moment. And to analyze these recordings, he had gathered a commission of five including Ellie. While Ellie and other scientists were analyzing the data sent to their PYXOMs, Ben had made a time travel and had been able to record the moment in micro second time frame.

Another message popped up on her screen. This was about a request to join the commission. She accepted the request right away. She had admitted she wouldn't be able to come to a conclusion by herself. But with the images Ben would provide, she could come up with new findings. She made a suggestion to include Naochi in the commission. The commission members welcomed her suggestion. Seconds later they started the virtual meeting.

"Thank you for your attendance," said Ben. "As you all know, in order to make time travel, all of us have to connect to a HISD device and the device has to be near us physically. Since there wasn't enough time, I was given a special dispensation from the Council to go to and record the time of the incident. By means of my recordings, in order to analyze the scene in three dimensions, we will not have an actual but a virtual travel to the time of the incident. If you like, we can start right away."

"Could you start the recordings ten seconds before it appeared Professor?" asked Ellie.

"Sure," said Ben, and in a few seconds, he completed his preparations. As the commission members approved, the virtual travel began.

All together, they watched the same scene; a white cloud coming out of a small hole, the cloud transforming into a balloon, the stranger appearing, the cloud going back to the hole and disappearing over and over. But they couldn't detect any anomalies.

"I would like to observe the time of this hole appearing and disappearing from the flat footage two more times," said Ellie and "if it is possible," she added.

Ben nodded and asked.

"Is there anybody else who wants to join Professor Ellie?"

The commission had decided to wait quietly, wondering what was in Ellie's mind.

"You can also follow the recording on your screens," said Ben and he made the necessary preparations to start the virtual travel.

After Ellie approved Ben to begin, she remained silent for a while.

Then, "Yes," she said.

"Look, right there," after Ellie marked it, a red dot appeared on everyone's screen.

"This is where the hole appeared," she added.

Then she marked the place where the hole disappeared with a blue dot.

"As you see, the spots it appears and disappears are not the same. Calculations indicate the incident lasted exactly nineteen seconds."

This time the image of the solar system and The Milky Way galaxy appeared on their screens. They made the necessary calculations by adding the speed of Earth's rotation, coordinates of the scene, time frame, and other variables.

"The spot of disappearance had to be right here, if the sun was compatible with our galaxy system," said Ellie and marked the spot with a yellow dot.

"Professor, can we examine the time of its appearance in slow motion one more time?" asked Ellie.

"Sure, I can slow it down a hundred million times and you can examine it in micro second frame," said Ben.

Starting with the time of the hole's appearance, the slow-motion images in the ratio of one millionth were flowing on the commissioners' screens. During the recording a chronometer was proceeding in microseconds. At 543.132.640 seconds the image extended then narrowed and returned to its normal size; while the image of the ground and the sky were vibrating, a dazzling flare appeared. This incident had only taken 5 micro seconds.

"Did you all see that?" asked Ellie.

Their eyes were locked on the screens with astonishment.

"Some sort of waving," said Naochi, keeping her eyes on the screen.

"Yes, the center of it seems to be that spot."

"I reviewed all the scanning device data we have but didn't come across anything. This waving seems like it never happened," said Ellie.

They looked at different spots on the Earth and in the universe, they had randomly picked on the same time frame of the incident. There had been the same vibrating and flare at those spots. The most interesting part of the situation was the detection of a wavelength they hadn't encountered before.

Ellie had completed her travel and started the calculations.

Everyone was silent; although they had the data before them, they couldn't generate a theory that would explain these incidents.

"There isn't a wavelength like this in scientific literature," said Naochi finally.

"Professor this is a great exploration. Congratulations."

"Thank you," said Ellie.

"At this moment we can only observe the incidents that happened at one millionth of seconds. If we could have examined this time frame not at micro seconds, but at one billionth or one trillionth of seconds, we would have found out more about the wavelength we couldn't identify. The results of what we have obtained so far— "

While the color wavelength scanner was running on, Ellie paused suddenly when she saw Naochi concentrating on her screen; Ellie looked at her screen, then after blinking a few times she turned and made eye contact with Naochi.

"Yes, it refers to solax frex. Also, gamma ray wavelength particles have been located."

"But," said Naochi excitedly.

"This is the frex and the wavelength that black holes diffuse," she added after a short pause.

"Do you mean that the stranger came to Earth through a black hole? But a human being going through a black hole is- - "

Naochi couldn't finish her sentence because the new data that had appeared on PYXOMs light screen had attracted her attention.

Ellie was looking at her screen without saying a word. She couldn't believe what she was seeing.

After ZA's identity could not be identified, his genetic scan had been made more sophisticated. The result of that scan was finally obtained.

The stranger didn't belong to the present. He was a person who had lived between 200 B.C and 100 A.D.

Ellie, Ben, Naochi and other commissioners examined the findings over and over without saying a word. Although they knew there wasn't a margin of error, they had difficulty understanding what they were reading.

Ellie got connected back to her PYXOM at the scene. ZA was walking up the hill, leaving the grove. She watched the stranger in silence for some time.

"This is impossible," she murmured, shaking her head. "Impossible!"

Until then she had been a scientist who had succeeded in solving many mysteries and making many explorations. But now, while looking at the biggest mystery of human history, all she could say was "impossible".

CHAPTER 8

ZA, who did not remember a thing, was looking around. He was trying to figure out where he was. He felt his head was empty.

Suddenly, he covered his genitals with his hands realizing he was naked. He made a full turn around himself. He looked around carefully and when he couldn't see anybody, he finally gave up covering his genitals.

He felt some things were odd. When had he got here? He wasn't able to gather his wits. His mind was all mixed up. He continued looking around. There were hills, trees, and plains. He did not know what to think.

Finally, he looked up. He saw a big white cloud in the middle of a blue sky. He was attracted by its decent shape. He looked down and this time he examined the trees and green grass more carefully. Everything was in perfect order. The tree branches were unusually symmetrical. He bent down and touched the grass. Every part of the grass felt the same; same length, same thickness, and the same texture. He was totally confused to see an untraditional kind of order dominating the nature.

"Where am I?" he asked himself while straightening.

"I wonder…I wonder if I'm in Heaven."

"If not, how did I come here? Where did I come from? How come I don't remember anything?"

He didn't move and waited for some time.

"This is a dream…It must be," he said to himself, but his answer wasn't enough to remove the puzzled expression on his face.

"I am in a dream, yes. Yes, this must be a dream," he repeated, murmuring like he was trying to convince himself.

This ambiguity, his blurry mind, unanswered questions, these were scaring him. He closed his eyes tightly to wake up from that dream. Then he gave up and opened them again. Even if this was a dream, it was a beautiful one to enjoy. He might not have the same dream again. There wasn't anything to be afraid of anyway. He felt himself secure and everything around him was so unreal to be this beautiful. If this was a dream, he was going to wake up sooner or later. He decided to enjoy it. Then he was filled with peace. The lines on his face relaxed and he smiled softly.

But soon the questions started crossing his mind again.

"OK, who am I?" he asked himself hopelessly this time. He stared far away. He forced himself to focus. He thought; he tried hard to remember but he could neither remember his name nor anything from his past.

He wondered if there were people living around. Would he be able to find them?

He looked up and shouted, "Aaaah!"

He waited.

He shouted again, "Aaaah!"

He waited.

He waited.

Then he decided to move on thinking no one was around. Perhaps he could find someone later.

But which direction should he go? He looked up, down, and around hoping to see a sign. There wasn't even a trail to follow.

No people living here? he thought desperately. All the questions in his mind were unanswered. He didn't know who he was. His only hope was to find other people.

"There must be somebody somewhere," he said to himself. He needed somebody to help him learn where he was and perhaps who he was.

While he was looking around, he saw a grove far ahead. He didn't know why, but a voice inside him told him to go there. He might have a chance to find a lake or a spring there. If there were people living here, they had to be close to water.

He walked for some time feeling the soft grass under his feet. He finally made it to the grove. The trees were not close to each other, but there were chirping sounds everywhere. Sunbeams were gliding through the branches, shining on the perfectly shaped grass and flowers where butterflies were flying over. He saw ivy on the tree trunk next to him and a fig tree a little further. He reached and pulled an ivy branch. Then he moved toward the fig tree and picked two large fig leaves. He tied their stems to the ivy branch tightly. Later, the leaves covering his genitals, he put the ivy branch around his waist and tied it. After checking its durableness by pulling on both ends, he felt relieved.
Am I used to doing this all the time? he wondered.

Was I wearing anything? Or was I always naked? Finally, he decided not to be naked because his uneasiness had faded away when he was covered.
Then why was I naked? he thought this time. But his question was unanswered again. No matter how hard he tried, he couldn't remember anything.

He felt pain in his crotch. He had to pee. He looked around; he didn't see anybody. He went under the fig tree and started peeing. He felt relaxed when he was done. He walked away from the tree pleased. He started thinking what to do next. While he was deciding which direction to take, he made a turn around himself to see his surroundings and suddenly was stunned by what he saw. The fig tree and other trees nearby had vanished. He blinked a couple of times then rubbed his eyes but nothing changed.

How can this be possible? he wondered.

What strange place is this? Where am I?

He finally gave up asking questions since none of them had been answered. He decided not to inquire into his situation. He headed toward the hills relying on his instincts.

CHAPTER 9

"Thank you for coming," said Gabriel.

"Hi Gabe! What are you showing me?" asked Ellie impatiently with a smile on her face and her eyes glowing.

Gabriel smiled back, then he looked from the corner of his eye at the men standing next to him. "These are my friends Nasir and Avram. And this is my childhood friend Ellie."

Avram almost extended his hand to Ellie but when he saw her saluting him with a head gesture, he pulled it back right away.

"Hello," said Ellie rather in a shy manner.

"I'm glad to meet you."

Gabriel's golden retriever dog Fanda was standing next to him as usual. Fanda seldom left

Gabriel and he was with him most of the time. He was looking at Ellie happily like he was trying to say, "Nice to see you again."

Fanda was a real living dog. The parasites that lived and fed on Fanda might have done harm to Ellie's health. Therefore, Ellie knew she had to stay away from Fanda, although she wanted to pet him so badly.

"Welcome," said Nasir and Avram one after another, smiling at Ellie.

They were both wearing white robes like Gabriel. But differently from him they were darker, shorter, and younger. Nasir was wearing a white taqiyah, a short-rounded skullcap and Avram had a black kippah, a brimless cap on his head.

Gabriel was her childhood friend and his name was Gabe then. After he decided to join the Believers, he changed his name to Gabriel. After that he became unpredictable for her. Ellie knew very little about his world and about these people.

After the end of the photon belt period, while humanity was wrapping its wounds, making progress in establishing new civilizations, religions had lost their ground. As a result of this, a very small population from all religions had come together and had chosen the holy land Jerusalem as their new settlement.

They obtained their food by cultivating soil, producing crops, and from dairy products like cheese and eggs. But they didn't consume meat.

The children born on this land had a free will to choose where to live after they were 12 years old. All Believers fulfilled their toilet and reproduction needs naturally. They called the other people in the commune Nonbelievers and they refused any kind of help from them unless there was a crucial matter.

Their land was covered with an invisible shield that didn't allow not only a bird but even a tiniest organism to enter. There were a lot of natural environments left like this for other colonies to live in all around the world. All living creatures under this invisible shield lived freely in their natural environments without any sort of interference. Ellie liked watching them; birds flying, dogs barking and the kids playing freely on the streets. On the other hand, there was an odd smell around she wasn't familiar with. She felt like she was on time travel when she was among these people who didn't use technology unless they had to. And from time to time, this feeling like being on a time travel made her uneasy. She didn't know why Gabriel had preferred to get old in these tough conditions. And also, she couldn't understand why he had chosen this life but not mutation.

Ellie heard a buzzing next to her ear. Then a fly got close. It almost touched her eye lashes, and when it was about to land on her face, it flew away quickly. Before she came here, she had had natural environment immunity coding onto her. She was safe. But this fly had come very close.

She wasn't used to this. She was about to lose her balance but the KRYXO under her feet didn't let this happen. At that moment, Gabriel had grabbed her by the elbow so that she wouldn't fall. When he saw she was doing fine, he took his hands off her. In a way he was apologizing because of his unnecessary move. Ellie responded him with a smile. When she felt Gabriel's strong hands touching her, this had made her whole-body tingle with joy. Her childhood memory appeared on her mind and suddenly she felt a desire to hug him like in the old days.

"Let's go then," said Gabriel, breaking the silence. He and his friends moved toward the bicycles leaning against the wall. Then he turned to Ellie.

"Byxroids have speeded up our work," he said. "It's because of you. We appreciate you, Ellie. I wanted you to see how much of a help you have been."

Ellie smiled at Gabriel.

Nasir and Avram were heading in front of them and Gabriel was cycling slowly next to Ellie. They passed by Jaffa gate after moving on one of Jerusalem's oldest streets, Omar Ben El-Hatab and arrived at Zedekiah cave. While Gabriel and his friends were getting off their bicycles, Ellie's eye caught the clock tower that was on top of a two-story stone building with a Bab El Jadid Street sign on it.

"This tower was built in the old ages by the Ottoman Sultan Abdul Hamid II," said Nasir, when he saw Ellie examining it closely.

"Later on, the site of the tower was changed for some reason. But we carried it back to its original place."

Ellie was listening to him trying to hide her skepticism.

"I mean, we didn't carry it of course," Avram interrupted. "Byxroids did all the work."

"I see," she said, smiling. Then she looked around.

"I haven't been here before. This place…" she said thoughtfully. She paused, trying to find the right word.

"This place is impressive. It's very nice that it was preserved for thousands of years."

Then they came to a square. After that, they entered the Zechariah cave through its narrow entrance.

Ellie looked around surprised. Byxroids were carrying big stone tablets. They had inscriptions on them and some were deformed.

"Where are we?" asked Ellie.

"Then the city was broken into," said Gabriel, gazing far away. "And all the men of war fled and went forth from the city at night by way of the gate between the two walls which was by the king's garden, though the Chaldeans were all around the city. And they went by way of the Arabah. But the army of the Chaldeans pursued the king and overtook Zedekiah in the plains of

Jericho, and all his army was scattered from him."

Ellie gave him a blank look.

"Yeremya 52:7,8," said Gabriel smiling.

Ellie continued staring at him. She had no idea what he was talking about.

"Well, don't bother," he continued.

"We are at King Solomon's quarry. King Solomon's temple stones came from here. This place is also known as the place where King Zedekiah hid after running away from Babylonians. The area of this place is 97,000 square feet. The length of it is 755 feet; although the depth is about 3.28 feet, in some places it takes up to 328 feet."

While Ellie was listening to Gabriel with interest, her PYXOM gave a signal for a call.

"Excuse me, I have to take this," she said while a blueish light came out from her white halo. It turned into a light screen going down her shoulders and stretching out to her KRYXO. It was Ben.

"Ellie, where are you?

"I'm in Jerusalem."

"Where?"

"At the Believers' land."

"There is state of alert, why did you go?"

"I just wanted to take a break."

He looked at her doubtfully. When she realized he wasn't satisfied with her answer, "To tell the truth," she continued. "I decided to wait for more data to come in because I couldn't reach a clear evaluation. I am with my friend Gabriel now and I think you will be interested in this place. Would you like to join us?"

"Sure," said Ben quickly. Ellie spending time with Gabriel during the state of alert had made him wonder about the level of their relationship.

"Could you wait for a second?" asked Ellie and she removed the blueish light screen by making it transparent.

"If you don't mind... Is it OK if Professor Ben joins us?"

Avram and Nasir approved it by nodding.

"Of course," said Gabriel.

As Ellie commanded, a small ring took off from the PYXOM over her head. It flew and came near her. Then it floated in the air stopping next to Ellie. Right after that, it reflected Ben's holomex appearance downward.

"Hello," said Gabriel.

"Hello. We greeted each other at school this morning but we didn't have chance to meet," said Ben. Then he turned to the others and greeted them with his head.

"I am Gabriel. Nice to meet you."

"And I am Nasir."

"My name is Avram. Welcome, Professor."

"Please call me Ben. Nice to meet you all," said Ben and looked around by making a complete turn around himself. "Isn't this King Solomon's quarry in Jerusalem?"

Gabriel nodded.

"I think the byxroids are carrying the Sumerian tablets," said Ben.

"Ages ago, an important organization called Free Masons had their first meetings at this quarry. The stones to Solomon's temple came from here. This place has some sort of significance for me because we can't travel to the period when Solomon's temple was built. More precisely, there are many time frames that are blackened. I mean for us, the historians, there are a lot of unraveled mysteries in the history of this place."

"The time period you are talking about is very important for us, the Believers. No one has revealed the secrets of King Solomon yet," said Gabriel in a monotone way.

"This blessing is given by God and not all of us can understand His blessing. He grants knowledge and truth to His servants he chooses," he added.

Ben looked at Gabriel for some time not knowing what to say. Although he knew a lot about religions, he wasn't expecting to talk to Gabriel about their beliefs. This situation made him uneasy but as a history professor he couldn't resist his desire for sharing his knowledge.

"There are assertions saying visitors from the Nibiru planet helped build the temple," said Ben calmly.

"This assumption has been widely accepted."

"There are so many mysteries waiting to be unraveled, right?" said Avram intervening.

130

Ben decided not to take it seriously although he sensed some sort of cynicism in his tone.

"Yes," he answered. "Like we have no trace of The Ark of the Covenant," he said.

"It's rather surprising to hear you mention The Ark of the Covenant," said Gabriel this time, smiling. Gabriel's eyes sparkling with interest hadn't escaped Ben's notice. Ben thought Gabriel was either hiding or not sharing some information on this issue. He could tell it from his smile.

"Perhaps this is coincidence or maybe fate," said Gabriel with enthusiasm. But today, you coming here and mentioning all these- - "

"Today?" Ben asked. "Is today a holy day for you?" There was a skeptic attitude in his voice.

"No, it's not but I just sense there is something special about today," answered Gabriel.

Ben and Ellie were looked at each other not understanding what he meant by those words.

"Well, in any case, it's nice to see you here," said Avram. Nasir nodded in a way that he agreed with Avram.

"Thank you," said Ben, then turned to Gabriel.

"Let's get back to The Ark of the Covenant. Do you know anything about that? Or perhaps you have found it?"

"Oh, no," said Gabriel. "If we had found it, you would definitely know that because the Ark of the Covenant will only appear with the return of the Messiah," said Gabriel.

"Yes, I know this belief," said Ben. Then he waited for a moment.

"Anyway, to be honest," he added, "I know it will be difficult to understand whether it is reality or myth when it's a matter of history of humanity. And to discover the reality, I wish the ark had appeared and I could see it with my own eyes."

Gabriel didn't say anything but just smiled and stared at him.

"All right," said Ben. He tried to escape from the looks and turned to Ellie.

"Why are you here?"

Instead of answering, Ellie turned and looked at Gabriel as if she was trying to say he was the reason for her to be there.

"I invited Ellie to our land," said Gabriel.

"I wanted to thank her and let her see the outcome of her help with her own eyes. She was the one who told me Byxroids could carry the stones with perfection. She even showed it to me on simulation so that I would be convinced to use Byxroids for this job."

"Nowadays, we've started to think technology was almost a good thing," said Avram smiling.

"Well, this tough job can't be done properly with manpower only," said Ben.

"So, have you heard about what happened recently? Have you heard about the visitor?"

After the men looked at one another, "Yes," said Nasir while the others nodded.

"We know about everything."

Ellie opened up her PYXOM's screen as the visitor was mentioned and started looking over the latest developments.

"We hadn't witnessed anything like this before," said Ben. "This stranger came out of nowhere. We still haven't determined where he came from."

"If you couldn't find where he came from using your technology, this must be a really extraordinary situation for you," said Avram, stressing the word "*extraordinary*".

"It really is," said Ellie to Avram keeping her eyes on her transparent light screen.

"We've encountered a big mystery."

"Have you been able to look over the latest developments, Ellie?" asked Ben.

"Some new data was updated right after you left. And most of it concerns your subject area."

"Yes, new information…" said Ellie. "There have been a lot of messages piled up. Well, this is unusual. I have to reply all but I have to look over the latest data first."

"Can I join you?" asked Gabriel, his eyes sparkling with interest.

"Sure," said Ellie with surprise. "But how will you connect to my PYXOM?"

"Very easy," said Gabriel smiling. Then he commanded, "Activate!"

And PYXOM emerged from Gabriel's back pocket. It stood over his head and from the same pocket a KRYXO got out and stood under his feet. Gabriel got on the KRYXO with two steps and looked at Ellie and Ben to indicate he was ready. Ellie and Ben watched him in surprise. Like Avram had said, the Believers seemed to like technology.

"Yes," said Gabriel looking at Ben and Ellie. "I'm ready."

"Fine," said Ellie. She had shaken off her surprised manner and looked at Gabriel's smiling face affectionately. Seeing Gabriel using technology had made her feel like the gap between the two was diminishing.

Ellie and Gabriels' long stare at each other had caught Ben's attention. Although this wasn't enough for him to comment on their relationship, it made him think there was a strong bond between them. They being childhood friends comforted him, but a voice inside told him this wasn't just an innocent relationship. Besides the uneasiness these thoughts gave him, they upset him as well even though he didn't have a clue.

Just when he was struggling with these uneasy thoughts, he saw a brown light flashing on their PYXOMs' light screens.

BROWN ALERT
BROWN ALERT
High risk of danger alarm code

CHAPTER 10

The reason for the alert was an unknown object that was located at a far distance in outer space. The image of the unknown object appeared on the corner of their screens. Underneath the image there was various data flowing about its speed, size, and its coordinates, etc. The most surprising data was its speed; it was 18,775 miles per second and it was moving on a straight line without having an orbit. This unknown object was given a name called ZZ. The calculations showed ZZ was moving toward the Earth at a high speed.

32:19:58:1505

On the left-hand side of their PYXOMs a countdown timer had appeared and a space craft closest to ZZ's route had been sent forward rapidly.

That was all the information for then. They had to stay put for new data to arrive.

This is just what we needed. First a human with an unidentified origin. Then an unknown object appearing suddenly. These two unusual events happening one after another in a short interval can't be coincidental, she thought.

"I need to speak to Naochi," Ellie said in a murmur. Then she looked at Gabriel.

"Do you mind if he joins us?" she asked, then she paused. "Or...I will have to speak to a few colleagues. Why don't we form a commission? I can help you join, Gabe."

"Well, I don't know," said Gabriel. "We don't belong to a commission like that."

"The Earth might be in danger. We must get rid of this threat. We have to minimize the risk by taking necessary precautions before it's too late," said Ellie.

"Maybe, you can provide assistance."

Ben was listening to Ellie in astonishment. How could the Believers be helpful in this kind of situation? Her proposal was proof that she was a lot more attached to Gabriel than he thought. And this attachment had affected her reasoning. Eventually, they needed a lot more than prayers in order to resolve the problem. But somehow

Ellie was thinking she could get his help. Or hiding behind this, she was trying to involve him in her life further.

He didn't want to oppose her proposal and provoke her. After all, the Believers couldn't be counted as members of the science commission. Therefore, they would be rejected kindly.

But at that moment, "There, they've been accepted," said Ellie excitedly. Then she turned to Nasir and Avram,

"You have PYXOMs right?"

Both men took out their PYXOMs and activated them.

Ben was watching the things going on in amazement.

"Yes," said Ellie.

"I've sent each one of you an invitation for participation in the science commission. Please accept it. Don't worry, we won't be too crowded together. At the meeting there will be three more specialists with us who have valuable backgrounds on black holes."

Nasir and Avram first looked at each other and then to Gabriel like they didn't know what to do. And when Gabriel gave his approval by nodding his head, they accepted the invitation. After that, Gabriel and Ben did the same.

Ellie had chosen a small lounge at Universal Science Institute for the commission meeting.

"Welcome," said Ellie after everyone sat down.

"Today, we have three guests: Gabriel, Nasir, and Avram. They are from the Believers' community."

The other three people in the lounge were surprised. They stared at the three men for some time. Then while they were saluting them with their heads, the Believers stood up and saluted them back.

"You know Professor Ben," Ellie added while Ben saluted them by blinking slowly.

"And these are my colleagues; Doctor Naochi, Professor Suen, and Professor Mark," said Ellie without a pause.

"I would like to get straight to the point since we are in a brown alert status," she continued.

"I'd like to start evaluating the data we have received recently. The object ZZ's starting point is a black hole twenty-three light years away," she said and reflected the image of the black hole with numbers and letters on its sides in the air.

"When we consider its speed, it will reach Earth a lot earlier than it should normally. As for its dimensions; it is 2329ft to 741 ft, its depth is 237 ft and its elliptical. It must have used worms to get here. ZZ reached here faster than the information we sent from its detection point in ovax format. We discovered that the Solax frex data that appeared with ZA belongs to the black hole ZZ came from. The most surprising is that both appeared challenging the principles of outer space and the laws of physics humanity has known so far. Although I feel a connection between them, I don't have enough data about the interactions their intersection points could create. Therefore, I couldn't analyze it deeply and couldn't come up with a theory."

Ben felt discomfort because he had thought the Believers joining the meeting wouldn't be helpful but when Ellie started talking, he realized he himself wouldn't be either.

"If you don't mind, I'd like to say a few things," said Naochi.

"The biggest source of uncertainty for us are the dimensions a black hole generates. These are very complicated and as far as we know each one of them is responsible for preserving the equilibrium in its own zone.

"Yes," said Ellie.

"Dimensions. I come to a dead end because there are so many unknowns about this subject. Then let's mention what we know about the black holes."

"A black hole releasing any kind of object is something that we had never witnessed before," said Suen.

"This isn't even possible theoretically. I mean, as far as we know. But it happened. What are we missing here?"

"Let's go back to dimensions," said Mark.

"Let's go through your theories. We assume that some dimensions can control photons. We also assume that all the movements in the universe are balanced with each other in an unmeasurable unit of a second. But we don't know how this occurs. If we assume those theories are real and since we know the universe does not administer balance with its reflexes, those must be the factors that are known and arranged before. Here from, "the universe knows the future" hypothesis can come out. Isn't it most likely for universe to have this sort of consciousness?"

After Mark stopped talking, Ellie caught Naochi's eye. Ellie had sensed it by her looks and expression that she was trying to say something but she was hesitating.

"Naochi," she said trying to encourage her. "Is there anything you want to add to Professor Mark's words?"

"Yes, what the professor mentioned reminded me of something." She paused and looked at Ellie and when she felt her support, she continued.

"The Perfect Universe Theory," she said

Ellie's green eyes twinkled.

"Could you summarize it for our guests?"

"Sure," said Naochi. After she gave a quick glance at the Believers, she turned to Ben and started explaining.

"According to this theory, the universe is rebuilding itself over and over in order to reach perfection by eliminating malfunctioning elements and correcting them in its system."

Ben sat up. This sounded very interesting to him.

"In other words, we might have experienced the same things over and over a couple of times," Naochi began. Then she continued.

"Well, there might be small differences in different versions. Until the universe reaches its perfect state, and until the new system becomes flawless, this rebuilding will continue. According to this theory, the universe resets itself again and again. For instance, sometimes people foresee the future a hundred percent correctly or reveal reincarnations with meditations. These are regarded as particles of error that shouldn't be in the system. This proves that the universe is still imperfect."

The lounge was silent. Ellie looked at Gabriel thinking he might want to say something, but instead she saw him restlessly moving in his seat. When he didn't say a word, she turned to Naochi, who was making some calculations.

"In summary," said Naochi. "I think we should consider this phenomenon as breaching of the principals made out of subtle balance in the universe. In a way, the universe might have decided to reset itself."

"Or, can there be a fuse mechanism that kicks in when an uncontrolled, unexpected energy is exposed into the universe?" asked Ben.

"What do you think, Ellie?"

"It's probable. Since the Big Bang, the formation of the universe hasn't been completed yet. The universe is still expanding," said Ellie.

It could be seen from her looks that she was impressed by Ben, since she wasn't expecting a question like that from him.

Everyone in the lounge started evaluating the data.

"Black holes might have been formed by the straining of the universe. They might also be the knots that hold the weak areas together," continued Naochi when no one objected. "The purpose of that straining might be to slow time or even to stop the universe to embrace perfection. For this reason, we should not ignore the conjecture that we might be living in a past time dimension."

When time concept was mentioned, Ben directed his attention to Naochi. But this didn't last long. He plunged back into his screen.

"The mathematics you use to explore the universe…" said Gabriel suddenly. Everyone in the lounge concentrated on his words. They were wondering what he would say next.

"Do you think we should examine mathematics?" asked Naochi.

"I don't want to cross the line. Science and math are your job, but I like philosophy," said Gabriel, smiling in embarrassment.

"And as you have decided to do brainstorming, philosophy might be the only thing that may cause a spark inside your immense knowledge," said Gabriel.

"Please continue," said Mark.

"For instance, there is no nothingness or emptiness in the universe but while analyzing it, the mathematics you use contains the concept of "zero". Isn't this a contradiction? Or not being able to observe a phenomenon called infinity. Have you ever thought why you can calculate all universe laws with slight deviations? Or why you can't demonstrate everything that you observe with mathematics and why you can't observe everything that you demonstrated with mathematics?"

"Did you mean these slight deviations originated from our mathematical system? If this is what you were trying to imply, can't these deviations originate from a hitch in the system?" asked Ellie to Gabriel.

"I just wanted to emphasize that you should question the methods you use to achieve your goals," answered Gabriel.

"It is very interesting that you make this comment," said Suen and then continued.

"I had studied the beliefs a while. For instance, it's been known that the urge to have sex was coded in the genes of living things so that they can reproduce. Although you know this as a Believer, don't you find it strange this urge exists without a cause in a surreal dimension you call heaven? Have you had an observation that would create an example with respect to this subject?

Contrasting ideas that hadn't been debated between the commune and the Believers for a long time had begun to develop again.

"No one has prevailed in this debate for ages," thought Ben.

"This is not the time for this argument," Ellie interrupted.

Nasir made a move toward Suen to answer her question.

Gabriel made a stop sign to Nasir with a hand gesture and turned to Suen.

"Oh yeah, I understood what you said. We also believe in things we can't demonstrate. While we call this faith, you name it science. Even though you examine and question, you take these contradictions as gospel. On the other hand, in our faith we adopt submission without questioning at some point. For this reason, let's leave aside the subject of faith for now. I believe it will be right for you to focus on the things you have been able to observe. There isn't anything called coincidence. We call this fate and you might call this something else. But if you believe every phenomenon has a reason and you can't come to a conclusion with the help of your calculation tools, I suggest you come to conclusions with the ones you observe instead of strongly attaching yourselves to your hypotheses," said Gabriel.

"Although I don't agree with everything you said, on some points I do," said Ben. He wanted to change the subject. Then he added, "I think there is an order behind this randomness. I assume a phenomenon called coincidence is an equilibrium mechanism of the universe to balance itself. As a history professor I have observed these many times. I think there are hypotheses in relation to that."

"Yes," said Ellie. "There are a few important hypotheses about the consciousness of the universe." Ellie was aware of Ben's intention to change the subject.

"We know that non-living objects are passive and living beings are active participants," said Suen. She also didn't want to take the argument any further. Especially when the Earth was face to face with big trouble.

"And we think all have efficiency coefficient that changes in one hundredth million of a second but this subject is in an area of many unknowns. If we could measure these coefficients, we might have unraveled the connection between ZA and ZZ easily," said Suen.

"You are right," said Naochi. "But we can't measure it. There might be a number of different dimensions we can't count. When we consider only about thousand of them have been analyzed, it can take us years to unravel this connection."

"Only a thousand? Are the dimensions that diverse? Can't you analyze all using a certain method?" asked Ben. He was curious.

"Unfortunately, no" said Naochi.

"It's impossible to adapt Gabriel's suggestion into this area. Because this is the area we don't have sufficient observation. That is to say, while analyzing a dimension with our special equipment, we observe that specific dimension can combine with another dimension within itself or with a separate dimension and can change dimensions again. In other words, some dimensions are not stable. We can't observe this change with our existing equipment. Although the moment of transition can be detected, in order to record in which dimension the deviation had occurred, all the probabilities have to be known. That means perhaps other undiscovered dimensions have to be identified. The complex structure of dimensions, the interaction web between them, their information flow and where, how and which mechanism the information was analyzed is a total enigma to us," said Naochi.

"I see," said Ben. He was embarrassed with his question because this had only caused a waste of time.

There was heavy silence in the lounge. Professors were still examining the data. Ellie was lost in thought. She couldn't come out of this chaos and each day she was losing hope that she could do it. It was as if all the experience and knowledge humanity owned had become worthless and the laws of an unknown, entirely different universe had been conducted. It was neither possible to predict what could happen next nor to understand what was happening. This was an unacceptable situation for Ellie. Perhaps Gabriel was right. There was nothing else they could do but to forget everything they knew and continue with observation. But they didn't have enough time for that.

"Excuse me," said Ben finally. He felt uneasy with his presence as the silence grew longer.

"Apparently. I won't be any help to you and therefore-"

"Please stay, Ben," said Gabriel.

Everyone looked at Gabriel.

"There is something I want to say. And if there is someone here to understand what I will say, that person is probably you."

Ben looked blankly at Gabriel.

"What do you mean? I am a historian, I don't know philosophy much."

"But you know the religions and beliefs, right? You talked about the Ark of the Covenant today. And I think this is a sign," said Gabriel.

"After the appearance of ZA, we also tried to understand what was happening," he continued.

"Nasir, I, and some mentors in our community brought up a probability today. Actually, this was not a subject we wanted to bring to you but when Ellie invited us to this commission, I interpreted this as another sign. I feel like I have to mention to you the probability we weren't even certain about. As I said before, the things you have said today, our encounter, and all these can't be coincidence," said Gabriel while looking Ben in the eye.

"Therefore, I believe I need your help. If the commission lets me, I would like to make a statement. Please, you should listen to this, too."

It was not possible for Ben to remain indifferent to Gabriel's words so he decided to stay.

"As I said, a couple of my friends and I have an idea on this issue, but we are not that sure you will be able to understand us. Actually, we don't think you would believe us." said Gabriel.

We need the tiniest piece of information and even an improbable hypothesis right now," said Ellie.

"All right then," said Gabriel, encouraged by Ellie's look. "We think ZA is the Messiah we were expecting." He had finally let the cat out of the box.

Everyone was quiet. All except Ben had blank expressions on their faces.

"Is that the one the Believers call Eesho or Messiah, the holy being that is expected to land on Earth?" asked Ben.

"Yes," said Gabriel. "Our Savior Jesus Messiah."

"This is not possible, Gabriel," said Ellie with a cold voice. She felt uncomfortable seeing her friend blindly depending on myths that had no scientific explanation.

"We don't expect you to believe us," said Nasir when he noticed Gabriel was frowning.

"But please make an evaluation before disregarding this probability."

"This Messiah, is that the person you mentioned during the Ark of the Covenant talk?" asked Ellie.

"Yes," said Nasir.

"Even if we accept this probability for a second," said Ellie, then hesitated.

"No, this can't be possible."

"Let's say you accepted that it is possible," said Gabriel. "What were you going to say?"

"Let's say this is possible… but this doesn't provide us any data to analyze it. Your hypothesis doesn't bring a solution to our problem. Let's suppose that ZA is your Eesho. You would take him to your land and live there pcaccfully altogether. And we would be pleased with this. On the other hand, we would continue our work to find out how he arrived here. But this is not the only mystery. What about ZZ? That it is coming from the same black hole as ZA. How are you going to explain this? Even if what you said is possible, this won't help us prevent ZZ from crashing into Earth."

"If what we say is the truth and even if you can't stop that object as scientists, you would have explored the truth. Besides, the reality of this means you don't have to stop the object. We've already told you that this person is The Savior, a holy being. Try to understand, Ellie; Messiah must have come here to prevent ZZ from crashing into Earth. He is here to save humanity."

"We are saying that they both came from the same black hole, Gabe. Suppose, ZA has a mission to save humanity and has supernatural powers to stop such a huge and fast object. Then why did ZA let that object come out of the black hole in the first place? If this is a holy being, why does he condone humanity experiencing this?

"Messiah will not only save us from ZZ, he will offer us the truth and this will bring freedom to humanity."

"Gabe… This…This is nonsense…" said Ellie.

Gabriel couldn't believe what Ellie had said. "Are you aware what you have just said?" said Gabriel, looking at Ellie, raising his eyebrows.

"You might not see a connection between these incidents and Messiah or not understand me at all, but this doesn't give you the right to call my way of life and what I underwent 'nonsense'. I am afraid I can't be in this meeting any longer," he said and before Ellie could respond, his holomex image disappeared.

"Excuse me," said Nasir after a moment of silence.

"We'd better go as well. Good bye," said Avram.

After Nasir and Avram's holomex images disappeared, a humming sound was heard in the commission.

"I guess I need to take a short break. I'll be back" said Ellie.

Then she turned to Ben. "I'm sorry, Ben, I'll call you as soon as I get back from Jerusalem," she said, smiling at him and ending the call.

As soon as she left the commission, Ellie looked around. Gabriel and his friends had already started moving toward the cave exit.

"Aren't you going to say bye to me Gabe?" she called after Gabriel.

Gabriel stopped and said something to his friends. While Nasir and Avram were moving away from Gabriel, he started walking toward Ellie. He was mad at her and he was trying hard not to lose his self-control.

"My name is not Gabe, that was long time ago, Ellie. It's Gabriel and you know that," he said sharply.

"Gabe is somewhere inside you. That is your past. Even though you change your name, wear those clothes, or have that long beard to your waist, you are my childhood friend Gabe and I can't forget him."

"Gabe became Gabriel, Ellie and this happened long time ago, but you just can't admit it."

"No," said Ellie. "This is not true. If it was, I wouldn't have set foot on this land."

"No, let's not deceive ourselves. If what you said was true, you wouldn't have that look in your eyes whenever we see each other."

"What look?"

"That arrogant look that says all my life is nonsense and asks when I would recover from my mistake, Ellie."

"I'm sorry," said Ellie when she realized how much she had hurt him. "I was wrong to use that word, you are right. I have no right to call a different way of thinking nonsense. I am a scientist and your beliefs don't adjust to the universal data."

"Weren't you the one who said you were open to all kinds of hypotheses because you could not explain how this object appeared with the data you had collected? Nevertheless, aren't you the ones playing God although you can't control everything?" said Gabriel.

Then he paused. He knew he had gone too far but the die was cast. There was no turning back and it was too late for any regrets.

"Just admit this," he said finally, softening his tone. "You are getting everything and everybody in your area under your control. But when you come across an unexpected or an extraordinary issue you begin to struggle. You are playing with your genes, wandering in different dimensions, but whenever you think you are close to playing God, you become aware that He is actually far away from you. You can't even cope with this simple truth. When you admit that you are only human beings and don't deny your incapabilities, maybe then you will be able to understand us and our beliefs."

"You are wrong at one thing," said Ellie in a calm manner.

"In our commune everyone might not believe in a creator, but all of us are aware that there are so many more mysteries to unravel in the universe. Therefore, we think the universe exists by means of an energy beyond human perception. On the contrary, we are trying to explore that creation energy, that creative power, or the architect of the universe, whatever you name it.

At least we are really making an effort for this cause. And you only try to get close to it without questioning. You are trying to do this by only worshipping with regard to the books you name holy."

"Since you think this way, then why did you invite us to participate in the commission meeting? Why did you prefer to spend your precious time with us?" asked Gabriel.

"Today is the time to act together. We want to make a coalition by combining our resources and potential."

"What about…What is your expectation from me?"

"I don't have any expectations from you. But you have some values that I can't make any sense of."

"What sort of values are those?"

"You proceed to death so willingly. Look at you and me. We are the same age, but while everyone can tell you are 150, I still have a young and healthy look. You refused genetic mutation and I just can't understand why you did that. Maybe death is the goal you want to reach." She hesitated and then continued.

"And what I want," she murmured.

When he sensed Ellie's sincerity, he didn't want her to finish.

"What you want might be a miracle, a phenomenon that doesn't fit into the principles of this universe," said Gabriel.

"And you've already met this miracle but you deny seeing it because of your prejudice."

She looked away from him.

"I don't care if you think it's nonsense," said Gabriel. "The person you call ZA can be the Messiah. The name you gave him actually refers to the Messiah."

"What do you mean?"

"Well, I'm sure you didn't give that name consciously."

"I don't understand."

"I am telling you; subconscious is in contact with conscious collectively. I mean it carries information codes of all humanity and this information comes to the surface when it has a chance," he said, and when he saw Ellie not opposing, he continued.

"The name you gave him, I mean ZA has a meaning in the Aramaic language, the mother tongue of Eesho that was spoken during that period. I see that you gave this name inspired by the information that comes from your collective conscious."

"Did you know ZA means magnificent, superb active light; Ziwa the masculine light form and shining sun?"

Ellie stared at him.

"Yes, Ellie, ZA might be the wall you want to run into. In my opinion, the thing you have to do is easier than what you think. You've tried your own methods until now and you couldn't get a result. We are requesting you to analyze ZA with our point of view. If you could do this unbiasedly toward us and our beliefs, I am sure you will be able to evaluate the connections that will emerge. After that, I will ask you to discuss your evaluation with us."

Ellie looked around for a few seconds before answering. She noticed that the bias she had against Gabriel when she was at the institute with her colleagues had disappeared when she was in Jerusalem. She was seriously thinking to carry out what Gabriel had said. Perhaps this place, and having this private conversation with Gabriel was affecting her judgement. Or maybe the reason thinking of this option was the desperation caused by the first alert. Even though hours had passed, she hadn't been able do anything about it.

"All right," she said finally. "This is completely a different field and I am unfamiliar with it. I can't do this by myself. I need to get Ben's support. I can do what you've said only if he supports me."

"I was going to ask you to do the same thing. I have no doubt Professor Ben will be a lot of help. But he will have his hands tied. You know that you can't time travel to the times of the prophets that are mentioned in holy books. This is because we, the Believers don't ratify it. So, I'll go ahead and get the permit for this time travel from my community as soon as possible. If you mention this while you are asking for the professor's help, I am sure he will be interested."

"All right then," said Ellie
"OK, bye."

CHAPTER 11

He was very hungry and thirsty. He was lying on his back. He tried to straighten up, but he couldn't. It was dusky, he wasn't able to see anything. He tried to focus, then he saw his hands, his tiny little hands and then his tiny feet. He was terrified. Those little hands, were they his? But how could this be possible? He tried to straighten up again; he struggled and tried to stand up but he couldn't succeed.

He looked at his hands and feet again. Was he trapped in a baby's body? How could this be?

Then he saw a face, a woman's face glowing in the dark. The woman got closer to him. She reached and picked him up. She held him between her arms and smiled at him with motherly affection.

Mother, he thought. He was surprised. She must have been his mother. She was so beautiful.

"Mom, who am I?" he wanted to ask. But no matter how hard he tried, he wasn't able to speak.

"I am here, Eesho. I am here with you," said the woman as if she heard him.

She had a soft, enchanting voice. He felt a glow of peacefulness.

The woman started to breastfeed him. His hunger and thirst had ceased and he was filled with happiness and peace. The desperation he had felt moments ago disappeared. He was so peaceful while getting fed in his mother's arms. He wasn't surprised anymore for being a baby.

After some time, his mother finished feeding. Then she lifted his head up and held him to her bosom. He could see her holding his tiny hands tightly. He didn't want his mom to let them go. He could stay there in her peaceful bosom forever.

After rubbing his back gently for a while, she put him back in his cradle. She covered him with his blanket affectionately and started to rock the cradle slowly. His eye lids were getting heavy and his mother's smiling face was vanishing slowly. He forced himself to keep his eyes open. He tried to resist sleep, sensing that he wouldn't see her again but he couldn't. His mother's face had already given its place to darkness.

He tried again and this time he was able to open his eyes. But he had to squint and then cover them with his hands because of the sun beating down on his face through the branches. This time he was surprised to have big hands. He wasn't a baby anymore. His mother had gone.

He looked around. He tried to understand what had happened but there wasn't anything remarkable to remember except his mother's glowing face. He had fallen asleep tired under a tree after wandering and looking for food and water, not knowing who he was and expecting to find someone in a foreign land. That's all he knew. And also, his name was Eesho. His mother had told him in his dream. It must have been true.

What if this was just a meaningless dream? he thought.

"This can't be," he said to himself. That must have been a memory from his past because the things he saw, he felt and his mother's affection were so real.

"Yes," he said to himself. "My name must be Eesho." He stood there like he was waiting for someone to confirm this.

"OK, who is Eesho?" he asked himself this time.

He couldn't get an answer.

He slowly stood up. He had to find something to eat, and most importantly he had to find water. He looked around while deciding what to do. Then something next to his foot caught his eye.

He was sure that it wasn't there before he went to sleep. He went one step back and slowly bent over. Whatever this was, it was very different from everything around him. He reached his hand to it hesitantly. He touched it softly with the tip of his index finger. It had soft tissue and it was round. It didn't look threatening. After a short hesitation, he picked it up. First, he turned it over and over, smelled it and then he examined it left to right, up and down, but he couldn't figure out what it was. Finally, he put it back on the ground.

CHAPTER 12

Gabriel had gone to talk to his community after he said goodbye to Ellie. Gabriel was going to ask Believers' Council for their consent to contact ZA and time travel permit to his time period. He was sure he would get their consent and permit because like he was, Nasir and Avram were also the members of the council. Nasir and Avram had already had their own groups' consent by talking to them. His group couldn't be saying "no". This was an extremely important subject matter for them. Sooner or later The Council was definitely going to open its door to the use of all kinds of technology and time travel to the forbidden periods. They had to make this sacrifice for humanity.

In the meantime, she had called Ben right away after she got on her FRYXO. She had told him what she and Gabriel had talked about.

Ben was absolutely happy to hear he could make a time travel to the forbidden time. This was a great opportunity for him. But he was very surprised when he heard about making contact with ZA. He almost thought Ellie had believed ZA was the Messiah. Yes, all his body data indicated that period but the important thing was not his identity. Eventually, he was an ordinary person who lived during that period. His name being Eesho or something else didn't mean anything for them and it shouldn't. Yet, the main point was how the visitor had arrived there. This wasn't a time travel. It was a direct leap and humanity didn't have that technology yet.

"Ellie, do you think we have time for that?" Ben said finally.

"The Earth is facing a huge threat and instead of analyzing the data, you say you prefer to make contact with ZA. Let the Believers do that part. Is it right to deprive Earth of your potential and your possible solutions? Are you sure about this?" he said.

"I understand what you mean, Ben. I can't say you are wrong. It's obvious I've come to a dead end."

"So, you choose to get help from myths when you come to a dead end?"

"I know this doesn't sound normal. But I have an intuition, Ben. My instincts that have always been behind my scientific success are directing me to think this way now. I know I will regret it if I don't listen to that voice. Don't misjudge me, I am not saying I believe the visitor is the Messiah. I just sense that I will find a clue I hadn't noticed before when I am investigating this assertion. And I don't want to ignore this possibility. Does that make sense to you?"

"Yes," said Ben. He really agreed with her at some point. But he was worried about Ellie that she might be interpreting her intuitions wrong. She might have been under the influence of her feelings to Gabriel when she thought she was listening to the voice that guided her to marvelous discoveries. And Ben couldn't solve this commitment exactly. However, it was impossible to turn his back on Ellie when she was asking for his help.

"You might be right," he said finally. "Seeing him in person and making contact with him might lead us to some answers. All right, I will help."

"Thank you," said Ellie. "I can't do this without your support. It won't take much of our time. We will just observe them when they are together. As a historian you can interpret their communication. We can also obtain exact dates from the period he is from. This will be worth our efforts. Our objective is not to persuade Gabriel. They can continue believing whatever they want. But I wanted to make contact with ZA anyway and by that I will have a chance to observe him. Perhaps I can find something that escaped our notice. I count on your foresight."

"Have you informed the Council? What do they think?" You know that they have to conduct this process."

"I wanted to speak to you first. I haven't informed them yet, but I will have a meeting with them soon," said Ellie.

No matter how certain Ellie was, Ben didn't think this procedure would be that easy.

As soon as Ellie ended the conversation, she sent a message to the Council. She reported that a few people from the Believers had decided to make contact with the visitor and also Professor Ben and herself wanted to join them in order to make observation. She didn't have enough time to mention the assertion of the Believers. She wouldn't have been able to do this even if she wanted to because she didn't think she understood their assertion well enough to explain to the Council.

While Ellie was waiting for the consent, a call appeared on her screen. This was Professor Diane, the representative of the Council. She had never seen her reply personally. Normally the top commission composed of committees would step in only in emergency situations if the commune people approved. The requests would be quickly evaluated, put to the vote of the commune people and the results would be directly reflected on the screen.

After a short hesitation, Ellie accepted the call. When she found Diane and other Council members looking at her with questioning eyes, she smiled, trying to hide her uneasiness.

"Ellie, we would like to talk to you about your request in person," said Diane. "We put your request to the vote. It's been rejected. Commune people think this might be a dangerous attempt. Well, we know that you don't have to comply with the decision. However, we hope you will act carefully."

"I understand. We could not find a way to stop ZZ at the committees we have formed. Moreover, there isn't a suggestion sent to the Council. We haven't yet determined the identity of ZA either. All in all, we don't have any concrete data. We need to make contact with ZA and I believe we should work with the Believers with respect to this issue. ZA might be the only alternative to stop ZZ. The data we have collected indicates ZA and ZZ are connected with each other. The data also supports that both of them have come from the same black hole."

"We know," said Diane. "We have examined your report and we agree with you."

"We have tried everything except communicating. I would like to observe him when he is with the Believers and, if possible, I'd like to ask him some questions. This might help us to connect the dots between ZZ and ZA."

"You know how irrational this possibility sounds. Despite the fact that we haven't found any other solutions, we don't approve this method either. You will join an unorganized society that chose to live in primitive conditions. You want to take uncalculated risks. As a commune we have not experienced death since the genetic mutation. If something happens to you, we can reproduce all your internal and external organs except your brain. And you know this very well. For this reason, the commune is worried about you and they don't want to put you in danger. Our world can be regarded as unimportant compared to human life. We can continue with our lives in other worlds but human life is indispensable for us. We have warned the Believers that this operation could be dangerous. They are also in favor of making contact with ZA. Well, we cannot prohibit you or them, of course. As a Council we can only make recommendations. But we must make sure you are aware of the dangers."

"Yes, I am aware of the possible dangers. I don't believe I will put the Earth and humanity under threat."

"You can only be responsible for yourself, Ellie. For the last time, I must let you know that making contact with the stranger is not approved by the Council or the commune people for the reason of endangering you. Do you understand this?"

"Yes, I do. Nevertheless, I must do this."

As a last resort, the Council representative Diane reflected the reacting messages of the commune people who were watching the meeting on their screen. Ellie could see the messages as well.

"For the first time, we are facing a decision that was voted against by the commune. Are you still decisive?" asked Diane.

Thousands of messages expressing worries for Ellie kept flowing on the screen.

Ellie was shaken and felt the utmost psychological pressure with these messages. As an experienced scientist, she shouldn't have been in turmoil. She had to be calm and had to proceed with determination. She was lost in thought. Diane was repeating her name.

"Ellie...Ellie."

Ellie finally heard Diane and turned to her.

"Yes, I am definite with my decision," she said.

"The commune is worried about your life and they are listening to you at the moment. Would you like to say something that would relieve their anxieties?"

The messages had stopped. Everyone was waiting for Ellie to say something.

Ellie hesitated with this sudden request. She thought about what to say. She moved her lips to say something but nothing came out. After a short pause she pulled herself together and decided to address the commune.

"Our ancestors not only put themselves in danger but made the supreme sacrifice for the future of humanity. I know that if necessary, every each one of you would also make this supreme sacrifice for the next generations. Our planet and humanity are under threat and none of the committees could make suggestions to unravel this mystery. I know the Believers are not organized at an advanced level. This is their life-style. This shouldn't be an obstruction for cooperating with them as a commune. I am aware of your anxiety for me and I am grateful. My decision is to cooperate with them. Don't interpret my decision as an opposition to the commune. If any of the committees or the commune have a new suggestion, they should reveal it right now. Every minute counts," she said and started waiting.

There was absolute silence. This situation had disburdened Ellie some. She had been relieved after she said what she had to. But her anxiety for the Earth and humanity still went on.

The silence gave place to messages from the commune. The pessimism Ellie felt before was left behind by the messages she saw. The new incoming messages supported Ellie. Under this circumstance, Diane intervened.

"In accordance with the recent developments, I would like to remind you that your contact will be observed closely. At any sign of danger, we will intervene in and ZA will be isolated. We hope no other risks will emerge and isolation will be sufficient. It is ultimately important that no harm comes to a living being no matter what happens."

"Besides, our PYXOMs, Byxroids and FRYXOs will be in the region. Also, we will speak to Professor Ben and inform him about the possible risks. Good luck to you for our planet and humanity," said Diane.

Ellie started to think after she ended the conversation. Did she really want this contact hoping to discover something, or had she accepted this to prevent a deeper gap between her and Gabriel?

She brought ZA's image back to her screen. He was sleeping under a tree. When the connection between ZA and ZZ was discovered, the "Aggressive Primitive" term for ZA had been changed to "Dangerous" by the Council. But the sleeping stranger looked totally harmless on her screen.

The PYXOMs in the region were still transferring data. All the nutrition his body needed had been determined. According to this, the Council had decided to prepare him a YUMXU. It was left next to him while he was sleeping. In the meantime, very interesting data was transferring; ZA was aging rapidly. His hair and beard were getting longer a lot faster than usual. His age had been calculated as twenty when he first appeared and now the data referred, he was in his thirties. For a reason no one knew, he was aging very fast.

Dr. Anne wanted to examine ZA closely. According to her, the data they had received couldn't have anything to do with reality.

"No living being in nature could undergo the aging process this fast," she said.

Nothing like this had ever happened throughout the history of the Earth. Therefor she sent an examination request to the Commune Council. The Council put her request to the vote. The answer was negative. Dr. Anne abided by the decision without a resistance.

Ellie saw ZA waking up. He looked around for a while before standing up. Then the stranger straightened slowly. The data showed his body lacked of vitamins and minerals. They were the life support units and essential for his good health. Ellie started watching him closely wondering how he would react to YUMXU when he saw it. YUMXU was a nutrient, a little bigger than the size of a tennis ball, filled with gel. The jelly melted when it combined with the enzymes in a mouth. When it got inside the mouth, this jelly ball that contained vitamins and minerals melted and became liquid. This was a way of getting nutrition for the commune people before they had the REST. It seemed ZA didn't know that YUMXU was a nutrient because he had first smelled it and then turned it around, turned it from left to right and finally he had put it back on the ground. This was not the behavior they were expecting.

Watching ZA had aroused her curiosity. Her gloomy mood had faded away. She was no longer affected by the stressful conversation she had with Diane. Her intuition kicked back in. She had to go there and make contact with him. But she thought it would be better if Ben didn't come. No matter how harmless ZA seemed, Diane was right. She had no right to involve Ben in this by putting him in danger for a reason she wasn't even sure about.

"I'm on my way," said Ben, as soon as she accepted his call.

"Go back, Ben," said Ellie in a self-assured manner.

"Why?"

"Haven't you spoken to the Council?

"Yes, I spoke to them moments ago."

"Did they mention the possible dangers of the contact?"

"Yes, very frankly and they were very insistent."

"That's why I want you to go back."

"I don't get it. You seemed very decisive. Was Diane able to convince you?"

"No, no. You have me wrong. I am going to the region. I just realized how wrong I was to ask you to do this. This is a risk I must take by myself."

"When I am there with you, it will reduce the risk factor you will undertake by yourself."

"No, listen, Ben, you must go back. Besides, you have never been together with the Believers in a physical environment. They have a very strong odor because they nourish in natural ways. You might be uncomfortable with it."

"If you are not going back, I am not going back. You've said it yourself; I am the only person to evaluate the Believers'contact with ZA. Let's stop the argument. We don't have much time."

"Ben, this is just not right."

"I don't think it's right for you go there by yourself."

"I won't be there by myself... Gabriel will be there, too."

He wasn't surprised but it was enough for him to be shaken by her answer He tried not to show his feelings.

"End of discussion," he said in a determined manner. "You've already involved me in this situation, and you need me as an unbiased observer to evaluate the happenings. As I told Diane, I am aware of the risks and I am ready to undertake them."

"But-"

"I haven't finished yet. Besides, it is important for me to be a part of this. You know that time travel to the times of the prophets was forbidden. But the Believers finally gave the permission. This means I will have the chance to enlighten those periods. I must support you on this subject. After all, this is the time for collaboration."

"All right. Do it as you like," said Ellie. "The Believers' Council is willing to act on the subject as well."

"This is great news. We will have more information on the subject soon. At least historic events will be brought to light. I'll do my best to help you find something. You can count on me," said Ben.

"If we can make this, it will be because of you, Ben. Thank you for your support, really."

Ben smiled. Her words were enough to ease his disappointment when she mentioned Gabriel moments ago."

"And also," said Ben. "Wait for me to get there. Don't try to communicate before I am there."

"OK," said Ellie, smiling. "Then hurry."

CHAPTER 13

The Believers' Council was following the developments. When they saw ZA was not eating the YUMXU prepared by the commune with Ellie's support, they received the approval of the Commune Council to send natural food. This food was to be delivered by the Believers' committee members that would make contact with ZA. A small committee was formed from seven women and one man. The committee's spokesperson was Gabriel. Each one of the members was to carry a PYXOM over their heads in order to be in contact with the Council and to be able to speak a common language. This way they would be able to communicate with ZA as well.

After making necessary preparations for communicating him and getting disinfected at the quarantine, the small committee departed with the vehicle called XFRYXO, which was a larger version of FRYXO carrying up to twenty passengers. They finally arrived at the region and saw ZA. In order not to scare him, they stopped their vehicle at a distance. Then they put the XFRYXO into invisible mode and stepped out.

ZA had seen them, too. This weird situation had made his heart race. All of a sudden people in white clothes had appeared in the middle of a plain. And now they were walking toward him. As they approached, he saw them carrying assorted food on trays. They all had halos over their heads. What sort of people were they?

Despite his surprise, instinctively he looked down and checked if the fig leave covering his genitals was still there. Even though he was embarrassed with his nudity, thinking that was the best he could do, he started walking toward them timidly.

"Stop there! Who are you?" ZA called with excitement when he was at a sufficient distance.

When Gabriel heard ZA speaking, this gave him a thrill. The language translation mode in their PYXOMs had been activated.

Everyone on the planet held their breath watching the contact on their PYXOM screens.

On the other hand, Ellie and Ben were still on their way to the region. Although Ellie was worried that the Believers had started the contact without them, she was relieved to see things going smoothly.

In the meantime, the language ZA had spoken was defined as Aramaic and it was quickly translated. After a short pause Gabriel said:

"Alaph, Beth, Gammal, Dalat, He, Waw, Zayin, Het, Tet, Yodh," and waited for ZA's reaction.

ZA was surprised at first, then he started murmuring.

"Kaph, Lammadh, Mim, Nun, Semkath, Ayin, Pe, Sadhe, Goph, Resh, Shin, Taw."

Gabriel and the committee members gave a happy smile realizing what this could mean.

Avram who was following the incident from his PYXOM turned to his friend Nasir;

"Gabriel made him say the Aramaic alphabet instead of the Hebrew."

When he saw Nasir looking at him, confused by his words, he continued speaking.

"In the old days the Jewish people living in and around Jerusalem spoke Aramaic as a second language to Hebrew. By this way, Gabriel determined what region and date he came from. This is great news. This shows we are on the right path."

"We have been appointed to make you comfortable," said Gabriel, as soon as it was reported the PYXOMs were ready to translate.

ZA noticed Gabriel's lips were not moving although the voice came from him. He wondered how that could happen. He wondered if these creatures were angels. Could he really be in heaven?

"Where am I?" asked ZA.

"We presume you are where you want to be."

ZA wasn't actually satisfied with this answer. He looked at Gabriel with doubt.

"What am I?"

"I see a human being before me."

"Have I died and is this heaven? Why can't I remember anything?"

"We don't know how and where you came from. But the only thing we know is you should not be here normally," said Gabriel.

ZA couldn't help himself looking at the food they had brought. There was bread, wine, honey, salt, cheese and eggs on the trays. He remembered how hungry he was.

One of the women laid a big picnic blanket in the shade of a tall tree. Then the women set the trays in the middle. They invited ZA by opening their arms widely and with smiles on their faces.

"Please enjoy the meal," said Gabriel.

"Join me. Let's eat together," said ZA keeping his eyes on the food.

"We are not hungry. All is for you," said Gabriel.

"Please join me anyway," said ZA.

After looking at each other, they sat around the picnic blanket making a circle.

ZA quickly reached out his hand to the food as soon as he sat on the blanket and started eating with great appetite.

"It's sad that you don't remember where you come from," said Gabriel.

ZA didn't say anything but nodded, his mouth full.

"Do you know who you are?"

"I don't remember anything," he said after he swallowed his food.

"You speak both Hebrew and Aramaic languages," said Gabriel.

"As I said, I don't remember anything, but I've had a dream. I don't know if it means anything …"

All of a sudden, he startled and stopped talking because two creatures had appeared very near them. These people that offered him food really looked like humans except with the halos over their heads. But the newcomers were very different from them. They were hairless and were wearing tight colorful clothes covering their bodies. They also had white halos over their heads, but the weirdest thing was they were moving in the air on a wheel-like horizontal vehicle.

When Gabriel noticed ZA was looking in a different direction with fear, he quickly turned the same way and then smiled when he saw Ellie and Ben.

"Don't worry, they are not strangers, they are our friends."

ZA looked at Gabriel not understanding.

"But," he said with surprise, "they look very different from you."

"Yes, but despite our differences, they are our friends. Don't worry."

"Welcome," said Gabriel standing up.

"Hello," said Ben. Then he turned to ZA. He wanted to say something to him but instead he just stared at him.

Ellie was observing the visitor, not looking away from him.

When Gabriel noticed ZA was worried, he said to Ellie and Ben "Please, sit down. I understand your worries for me. I appreciate it," he said smiling at Ellie.

Ellie and Ben looked at one another not knowing what to do. Then Ellie sat in the space that was reserved for them without getting off her KRYXO, but she looked anxious.

"Dear Ben," said Gabriel, turning and smiling to Ben. "We are very lucky to have you here. Thank you for coming. Please sit down."

Ben didn't say anything, he just nodded. After a moment of hesitation, he also sat down without getting off his KRYXO. After that, Gabriel took his place and sat back next to ZA.

A scientist and a history academician sitting around a picnic blanket with ZA and the Believers was an extraordinary view. All humanity was watching this with great surprise.

Meanwhile, Ellie didn't want to miss any updated data so she quickly activated her screen.

When the screen came down from her PYXOM, ZA startled again.

"Our friends use some different devices but they are totally peaceful and harmless people," said Gabriel. "Do not worry. You are safe with us."

"Are they human too?"

"Yes, of course," said Gabriel, smiling.

"What kind of a world is this?" said ZA, mumbling. "I don't remember where I came from. But I am sure I have never been in a place like this."

"Don't you remember anything?" asked Ben in Aramaic language, eventually.

"No."

"Don't you know anything about yourself?" Ellie asked.

ZA noticed Ellie and Ben weren't moving their lips when they were talking either.

"All I know is I found myself here. And I felt very hungry and tired. Therefore, thank you very much for sharing your food with me."

"This is our pleasure," said Gabriel, his eyes sparkling.

"Isn't there anything you remember?" asked Ben impatiently.

"E-LEE L-MAA-NAA SAA-BAACH-TAA-NEE," said ZA.

"Only these words. They are not getting out of my mind."

A flash had appeared in the eyes of the Believers when they heard his words but then it left its place to sorrow. They all knew the meaning of these words very well. These were the last words of Eesho when he was crucified;

"My God, my God why have you forsaken me!"

They waited, holding their breath. They couldn't have told him that those were his last words and why he had remembered them.

Ben also turned on his screen and started searching. His PYXOM had translated ZA's words. He knew ZA was speaking Aramaic language, but his last words didn't make any sense to him.

Aramaic language was integrated with Syriac and was similar to Hebrew, but an older language than that. Its roots went back to Edessa, an ancient city in Anatolia. At the same time, it was the mother tongue of Eesho who lived between 200 B.C. and 100 A.D. Ben hadn't reached extra information or the information that would disprove his knowledge.

He didn't want to lose much time. He couldn't wait to travel to forbidden times to deepen his research. This was a sensation he hadn't felt for a long time. Having a child was even insignificant compared to this enthusiasm. He was going to be the person who would uncover the truth about the religions and make a historical discovery. He was going to prove to the whole world that the religions were made up of myths.

While he was enthusiastic about this, all of a sudden, he felt anxious. He remembered the desperation Earth was in. Perhaps he shouldn't have been this much biased. Perhaps the Earth was going to perish before he made his discovery.

He continued his research, trying to escape from these negative thoughts. Just then, an extremely striking information appeared on his screen. The words ZA had uttered were the last words of Eesho. He was completely baffled with this finding. How could this be possible?

"No," he said to himself, this had to have another meaning. ZA using an ancient language was making him already think he might have leaped from the past. But him, uttering those words didn't prove he was Eesho. Perhaps he was one of the Believers and before he came here, he had had a bad experience that he couldn't remember now. This and many more probabilities could possibly explain why ZA had uttered those words

Ben saw Ellie getting up on her KRYXO and going toward her FRYXO while he was lost in thought.

When he got up to understand what was going on, he saw Gabriel doing the same.

"What happened?" Ben asked when he got near Ellie.

"This is all nonsense," said Ellie lowering her voice and pointing to the picnic area with her head.

Just then, Gabriel came near them.

"What's going on, Ellie?" he asked.

"I'm sorry Gabriel but I am a scientist and an unknown object is approaching Earth at a great speed. So, it is not rational for me to sit there and chat right at this moment. I could not receive satisfactory or soothing answers to my questions. How can we find a solution to a problem by having a picnic?"

"I can't say you are wrong," said Gabriel when they all stopped at a distance from ZA.

"Do you really think so?" asked Ellie with surprise.

"I wasn't really expecting him to remember anything," said Gabriel.

"This has been disappointing for us and of course for humanity as well. Besides that, I know you don't belong here and I respect that. Thank you for your sacrifice. But still," he paused and then continued.

"If I were you, I wouldn't call all of this irrational." He gave Ellie an implicit look right after his words.

"All in all, it was worth trying. But I agree that we haven't got a solution for now. Even though I want to be with ZA right now, it's obvious we can't get anywhere by sitting and chatting. Even for me, I feel this is not the place where I should be."

"What do you suggest?" asked Ben.

"I think there is no need to delay that time travel."

"This is what I was expecting," said Ben smiling.

"Is Gabriel joining the time travel?" asked Ellie, not hiding her surprise.

"Yes," said Ben. "Their Council gave consent only if a mentor from the Believers accompanied me."

"I see, but…" she said turning to Gabriel. "this is something very big. I mean, I thought using highly developed technology and making time travels were against your belief."

"Actually, not exactly. We are not turning our backs on technology or science. We only think it's not right to use it unnecessarily, to carry on our lives with the help of it or to rely on it. We are only trying not to act against our nature. Besides, there is a critical situation now and our faith supports using technology for the sake of humanity," said Gabriel. But the answer he gave hadn't prevented him stopping the thoughts that sometimes came into his mind.

Why didn't I give an honest answer? Why have we never investigated our past? Reality stays in the past. All right, we never investigated, but why didn't we allow the commune to do this? I wonder if the past is different than what we think or the way it was presented to us. Why did we stay away from our past? What if the reality is different? Then I would feel myself weightless and naked. Maybe my subconscious is acting cautiously by not allowing the investigation of the past. Why can't I be transparent like Ellie and Ben? Aren't the boundaries too broad for obeying the unknown in our faiths? Gabriel suddenly stopped thinking. Was the devil playing a game on him?

God must be testing my faith. I mustn't have such doubtful thoughts. I'm on the wrong path. I'm definitely on the wrong path. God forgive me for questioning your sovereignty. The gaps in Gabriel's thoughts had been filled in by some sort of instructions guide that kicked in like a fuse in the systematic of faith.

When Ben saw Gabriel hesitating, "Let's not lose any more time and clarify the details," he said looking at Gabriel.

"Even if we assume we are looking for someone named Eesho, this will take us more time to come to a conclusion without a certain procedure. I am not sure where to start while the settlement is widespread, Eesho's life; where and when he lived is unknown. We can start our search from the city of Edessa in Anatolia."

"Even if we come to a conclusion, it's going to take a long time," said Gabriel in a thoughtful manner.

"I suggest we go to the temples in the region. Eesho was a Jew at first. And as far as I know, the Jews of those times used to gather at the temples on Fridays to worship and socialize," said Ben

"Shall we start with this plan? But we still need to scan a 300-year time period between 200 B.C. and 100 A.D. What do you say?" added Ben.

"Would you like me to narrow this time frame a little?" asked Gabriel. His eyes were shining.

"How will you do that?" asked Ben.

"We know that the old calendar starts with the birth of Eesho. Well at that period, there wasn't any record of birth or death. Therefore, how many years Eesho lived is uncertain. They mention ages 35, 38 and 40. Also he was considered to be baptized at the ages between 30-35. Well I think he was baptized at 33 because many years after Eesho's death, in the old Roman Catholic Church, the priest coats had 33 buttons and they used to fasten them with prayers. Even, some churches rang their bells 33 times in those periods."

Ben was listening to Gabriel, feeling uneasy because of giving him the controls on the subject.

"And all these are assumptions," Ben said finally.

Because of his interest in this subject Ben had made a research. It seemed like it was working now. Focusing deeper on the subject, receiving information from the Believers and providing some to them made him extremely satisfied and happy.

"There is no concrete evidence that the old calendar started with the birth of Eesho," added Ben.

"Is that what you think?" asked Gabriel, and stared at Ben for some time.

"All right, as a historian if you are looking for concrete evidence, I suggest you to make a travel to Jerusalem to year zero. You need to locate Eesho in his childhood because he's known as a traveler during his adulthood. Since his birth is a very important phenomenon, it is impossible for us to miss his existence during our travels. Even if I'm wrong, at the end of our travel you will be certifying if all the information reached to the present day has basis or not. I think we can satisfy our curiosity only by this way. What do you think?" he asked with excitement.

"All right," said Ben, with a vague smile on his face.

"Then, I must warn you about the dizziness that you will experience during our travel."

"No problem," said Gabriel smiling at Ben.

"Let's keep going then. The nearest HISD is at the university. We will review the details on our way."

"OK, but what about ZA?" asked Ellie.

Gabriel turned around and looked at ZA, who was sitting on the blanket and tucking away the food.

"He looks fine," he said. "There is nothing we can do for him for now. I'll ask the Council to send a couple of people here. You are watching here as a commune as well. The ladies at the picnic area are our valuable mentors. I believe they can handle any problems that occur."

"So, let's not waste time," said Ben. "We've already lost a lot of time."

"I'll stay here," said Ellie.

"Why?" asked Gabriel with surprise. "You've just said you didn't belong here, didn't you?"

"I mean when I said here, I didn't mean I would stay here with your friends," said Ellie, in a thoughtful manner.

"There have been some new developments and I'm planning to sit here in my FRYXO and make some calls and do some calculations. I will evaluate the information and then decide what to do."

"I haven't heard about the recent developments. What sort of developments has there been?" asked Ben excitedly.

"There are a few possible contingencies, really," said Ellie. "Like destroying ZZ before it enters the atmosphere…And as you know this is an alternative we never wished to consider. However, I 've obtained information that this alternative might come up in the Council."

While Ellie was moving towards her FRYXO, Gabriel called after her.

"Take care, Ellie!"

Ellie turned and looked at both men, smiling, not saying a word. Then she moved on.

After Ellie got out of sight, Ben turned to Gabriel. When he saw his eyes shining, he had no doubt his eyes looked the same. Gabriel was going to make a time travel to the center of his faith that he devoted himself to. He was going to visit the land he knew was holy and the land he was living now.

CHAPTER 14

After Gabriel and Ben left, Ellie got on to her FRYXO and before making any calls had started reviewing her calculations hoping an idea would appear in her mind. But the countdown timer on her PYXOM screen was distracting her.

31:20:00:1201

She looked at the changing numbers for some time.

"How are we going to stop you?" she asked to herself.

The information about ZZ continued showing up. She had no other way but to evaluate all data from the beginning using the recent information.

The unidentified object was proceeding on a straight line at a constant speed without being affected by any planets' gravitational field. The new images had proved that it had a different structure than a meteor and it wasn't something they could identify. It was a color changing elliptical-shaped object made of large and small spheres.

Was this a natural object? Or was it a man-made spacecraft? If this was a spacecraft, could there be any kind of living-beings in it? Despite all kinds of calculations being made and all efforts to contact it in order to obtain information, no signal or data flow was recorded from the object.

While Ellie was evaluating the data, suddenly new information appeared on her screen stating that the object had disappeared. She was indecisive about how to describe this unexpected development right when she was making a more detailed scan of the previous data. Nevertheless, she continued with her calculations to explain the situation like every scientist.

She received a call from her assistant, Naochi.

"Did you see that, too?" asked Naochi.

"Yes."

Naochi shared the images on her screen with Ellie.

"Right at that point, the object went into a time travel worm that appeared unexpectedly."

"Are these the worms that we can't detect their place and time?"

"Yes."

Naochi continued, explaining the image she reflected on the screen.

"We analyzed the moment of disappearance at 550 different frex sequences but we lost track of it."

"Now, look"

In front of the object, Ellie observed a multicolored time wormhole that was around 0.7 inches in diameters. This worm was a throat connecting two mouths and it had expanded in a size to swallow the object. This multicolored throat had appeared less than a second before the object had got into it. As soon as the mouth closed, the image of both had disappeared in space.

"Which data base did you use?" asked Ellie.

"It was formed by overlapping the frex combinations; Fez8, Yar49 and Ner2."

"This can't be a coincidence. When you observe its position and the timing, it can be understood that this was planned," said Ellie and added,

"Then what was the factor for the object and the worm to operate with exact coincidence in time?"

Neither of them had an answer to that question.

"Could there be a communication link between them? Let's share this information with the other commissions via the Council."

Naochi nodded and again she looked at the images and numbers that changed continuously on her light screen.

Ellie was overwhelmed with unanswered questions. She lifted her head and looked outside from her FRYXO. ZA had worn a white robe and he was sitting on the grass with the Believers. "The Earth might be destroyed in hours but they don't care a bit," Ellie thought looking at the happy expression on the Believers' faces.

She zoomed in her lens on ZA's eyes and questions ran through her mind.

Who are you? What are you? Why are you here?

"What am I doing?" she asked herself. "This is aggressiveness." This strange urge had really started to worry her.

She remembered what the doctor had said. The side effects of the treatment were so severe that Ellie was afraid to lose her control at some point. It was not possible to use any sort of tranquilizer under these circumstances because she was afraid this could prevent her from using her cognitive skills. But what was she going to do?

What did she use to do when she couldn't find answers? First of all, she wasn't aggressive like this. Actually, the Earth had never been in danger like this before. But again, she was absolutely sure that normally she would be calmer than now.

She looked outside at ZA again. His sharp eyes looked tired now. His physical appearance was slowly changing compared to the time of his arrival. This human being was getting old fast in front of them. But no one could explain this or the unidentified object using wormholes.

She had to be rational and calm again. She had to be the person everyone knew before; she had to be herself. Spending time with Gabriel had also shaken her as much as the side effects of her treatment. She could feel it. When she spent time with him, she felt like the doors in her brain were shutting down one by one and emotions were taking control of her.

She was amazed by the Believers' relaxed mood. In fact, she secretly envied them. Perhaps she wanted to be like them. Even though Earth was on the verge of extinction, sometimes she thought of giving up the struggle, accepting all that had happened and spending her last moments on the Earth with Gabriel.

"Maybe we won't be able to find a solution," she said to herself.

This might be happening to her because of this huge threat or the side effects of her treatment. She was getting carried away easily and more_ over she was trying to normalize thinking like this.

Nevertheless, she was aware that this type of thinking was not normal at all. She had started to be afraid of the thoughts crossing her mind. Therefore, it was time to enable the absolute reasoning.

"No," she said finally.

"All these thoughts in my mind are because of my treatment," she said, trying to convince herself. Giving up and surrendering were not for her. These were the type of behaviors the Believers would show and she was a scientist. She had to dedicate her knowledge and experience to humanity. She had to use all of her capacity for saving the planet. This was her fundamental duty that she valued above all things.

Maybe she had to stay away from Gabriel until this situation was resolved.

Fortunately, he is not here. He is working with Ben, she thought. Then suddenly she panicked. "Even Gabriel is trying to find a clue to save the planet. What about me? What am I doing?" she asked herself.

Even Gabriel is using technology and he's not hesitating to do this. Here I am thinking of quitting and giving up everything. And with Gabriel beside me watching the Earth, my home being destroyed is crossing my mind, she thought.

These thoughts were disturbing and they were enough for her to come to her senses. She shouldn't have spent her time fantasizing these pointless things. She turned and looked at ZA's tired eyes.

"We will find out who you are. Even if this is the last thing we do, we will stop that object," she said to herself.

"Professor," replied Naochi to Ellie's call.

"I wanted to talk to you, too" said Naochi.

"Is there a new development?" asked Ellie.

"No," said Naochi.

"Then, I am suggesting a small meeting to analyze the latest data. What do you say Naochi?"

"I say let's do it right away. Who shall we call?"

"Professor Diane and Professor Kelly."

Professor Kelly was specialized in unidentified objects and the spokeswoman of the spacecraft commission. At the same time, she was the head pilot of spacecraft fleet.

In ten seconds, all had joined the virtual meeting at the lounge of Universal Science Institute.

This is where I belong, thought Ellie while looking around. Asking the right questions would help them to get the right answers. She was going to try to create a solution with the others here. They had to and she believed they could do this.

"As we have observed, contacting ZA was not a solution," said Diane.

"Have you run across anything that would support the connection between ZA and ZZ, Ellie?" asked Diane.

"No, I haven't. The stranger doesn't know who he is, where he is from or why he is here. There is nothing else that we have observed so far. I was wrong to think we could find a clue."

"Are there any new findings about ZZ?" asked Diane, turning to Kerry.

"All I can say is it acts like an object with a purpose, using the wormhole and not getting into the gravitational field of other big space objects proves that. It disappeared four minutes and-" she looked at her screen then continued, "eighteen seconds ago. Since then we haven't found anything new."

"I think this object is a spacecraft," said Kelly.

"Do you think there is a living being or beings inside the object?"

"There might be. Also, it is possible that it could be controlled by something. But I think the third option is more possible."

"You mean?" said Ellie.

"It might have consciousness. Well, of course, it's more likely that it might have been created with artificial consciousness. I think the object consciously protected itself from being scanned using a sort of shield. This shield might not have been activated during the first scan. Because the information flow suddenly stopped two seconds after the first data was received. It disappeared inside the time travel wormhole just when our space station had reached the region to make a detailed scan. Well, there might be living beings inside the object as well," and Kelly continued. "They might have noticed us and taken measures. If so, they must be either very different beings or more developed than us since they took a risk to get into the wormhole. On the other hand, we should consider the possibility that there might not be living beings inside this object. As I mentioned before, this could be a spacecraft equipped with high technology and it might have artificial consciousness."

"We are having difficulty finding a solution to the problem because we only have hypotheses. We must have more data. We must have an answer to the question "why an unidentified object with consciousness is traveling to our planet at full speed?" said Ellie.

"This can be a discovery spacecraft," added Ellie.

"A spacecraft that came from far space. But..." she said than hesitated. She made eye contact with everyone in the meeting and then continued.

"Its structure makes me think that it is not a peace-loving object."

"What data is making you think this way?" asked Diane.

"When I saw that sphereball made of big and small spheres joined together, I set aside all data and focused on the object. I realized it was an object controlled by different beings when we noticed it was not affected by the gravitational field of other planets. In that case, it wasn't a natural formation and its structure had to be serving a purpose. Look at our planet, our peace-loving technology; none of our spacecrafts have a shape like this. Isn't that correct, Professor Diane?" said Ellie.

Diane nodded and Ellie continued.

"The structure of this object indicates that it might have different intentions toward our planet. When it reaches the Earth's surface, we all know that there will be a collision. After the collision the spheres might spread to different points to collect data for invasion. Or they might be some sort of mechanical devices in the form of spheres that will transform into war machines to start an invasion. If there are any living beings on the Earth's surface during this collision, they definitely won't survive. It is less likely that this object is friendly," said Ellie. After a short pause, she continued.

"The boundaries of our imagination consist of combinations of events we already know in the universe. We don't know what we don't know. Could this object be a different form of subatomic particles? For your information, there has been more than five hundred subatomic particles discovered and are still being discovered. Some of them move parallel to the dimensions. We try to push the boundaries, in other words, we try to expand our horizons but we are not able to do it," said Ellie.

"It might slow down before it reaches the Earth," said Diane. "It might be coming for a good purpose."

"If you excuse me, I will interrupt. If it was like that, they wouldn't have gotten into the wormhole despite our efforts to communicate with them," said Naochi.

"Also, they would have communicated with us and notified us about their friendly visit."

"The wormhole…" said Ellie.

"Perhaps it has this shape to make it easier when entering the wormhole."

"Another possibility is they might have a plan to invade after we evacuate the Earth," said Diane.

"What about ZA?" asked Ellie. "What could be the connection between them? Why would a creature like this come to the Earth before an invasion?"

"The data we have obtained about this creature supports he might belong to someplace else in the past. This might not be the first attack to our planet. After all, even with history travels we cannot find out what happened during the blackened periods. We could have focused more on the object if there wasn't ZA. His presence has quite distracted us," said Diane.

Ellie didn't say anything for a while. She thought she had to reach Ben as soon as possible and have his opinion about these hypotheses. This subject was in his area as well.

"I don't know Diane," said Ellie finally, raising an eyebrow. She looked thoughtful.

"We can create hundreds of hypotheses."

It was hard for them to accept the hypothesis that the object was coming to Earth for invasion.

This was something they didn't even want to think about.

Diane looked as if she wanted to say something but before she could express her opinion their PYXOM light screens started to flash. It was the brown alert image flashing onto the screens.

The alert was sent from the space station that had done the scanning of ZZ. It said an unidentified object had appeared somewhere in space. This was exactly the same object that had disappeared seven minutes ago. ZZ was back and it was approaching Earth at full speed.

The countdown timer appeared on top left corner of their screens once again.

27:19:59:0101

It had covered almost a four-hour distance in seven minutes.

The information continued to flow from space. A map flashed onto their screens. The coordinates of its collision point to the Earth had been calculated. This was the spot where ZA had appeared.

"All these can't be coincidence," said Kelly, shaking her head.

"Collision simulation!" commanded Ellie. This time she was not able to hide the excitement in her voice, but no one had found this strange because they were all very much concentrated on their screens.

The simulation referred to one finding: the extinction of life on Earth.

"It's time to accept we couldn't succeed in identifying this object. We must change its route before it hits the Earth. If this won't work, we should take it apart to decrease the effect of collision. If we can't succeed in that either, we should try to destroy it," said Ellie. Although she sounded calm, it didn't escape Diane's attention that her eyeballs had gotten bigger.

"I agree. The first thing we should do is to change its route. If we can't succeed in that, there is no other option but to destroy it," said Kelly.

"Just in case, we should focus on how to attain the strongest effect against it," said Ellie.

"Do you mean the Fusionuc Power when you say the strongest effect?" asked Diane, lifting her eyebrows. She paused for a second. "You mean the filthiest technology in the history of mankind that consists of nuclear power?" she added. "I think we shouldn't bring up the idea of using Fusionuc Power for now."

"Let's say we did all we could to stop it but we couldn't succeed...Then what happens? We can't leave anything to chance. I am following the other commissions as well. Neither of them has come up with any solutions in their discussions yet. I will suggest the Council to carry out the evacuation procedure of Earth as soon as possible. Our Moon base seems to be the biggest to host the most lives."

"This is the last scenario we should insist on. Right now, we should focus on our first option; changing its route. However, this option has not been mentioned in any of the commissions," said Kelly thoughtfully.

Naochi interrupted.

"We cannot determine how intense the collision effect to the Moon will be after the object crashing to the Earth. We don't know what this object is made of. It might be carrying an energy a lot more destructive than nuclear."

They played the simulation in different variations. There was no doubt that the object crashing to Earth either as a whole or in pieces would cause a huge damage and the Moon would be affected by this collision. Besides, there was a probability that the Moon's orbit would change as well. However, a sudden change was not expected. But the main issue was that the simulation could not calculate the amount of mass the Earth would lose. Naochi was right about this; they had to have more information about the object.

"Anyway, this is our only way," said Ellie.

"It is risky, but we have a chance," she added.

"If this object is not any kind of a destruction weapon, the masses that will break off from the Earth won't be big in size. Then, the Earth's gravitational field will prevent the Moon's destruction. And also, during the collision the Moon will be on the other side of the Earth's surface" said Naochi.

"How long will it take the expansion of the bases to provide new living areas?" asked Ellie.

Diane, who was still making calculations on her screen, answered Ellie's question.

"Our calculations say at least ninety-six hours."

"Life support units at the space colonies, do they meet the requirement of ninety-six hour waiting time?" asked Ellie.

"I am checking." Naochi looked at the results on her light screen and added.

"Yes, they do. Up to 120 hours," she answered.

"We should suggest that the Council start the expansion of the bases right away," said Ellie.

Kelly and others nodded, confirming what she said.

Upon that, Diane sent a letter to the Council suggesting the expansion of the closest bases in outer space and on the Moon. So that they could start the evacuation process right away before the collision. Also, proper conditions had to be provided to preserve the DNA of all species. After the evacuation of Earth and people being transported to outer space, the Byxroids could continue working on the expansion of the living areas on the bases. Later on, the damage and risks on the Earth's surface would be calculated and a new action plan could be formed.

After a short wait, the Council replied to Diane. The preparations had already been started as soon as ZZ had appeared. As a first thing the capacity of life support units in all colonies close to Earth had been checked. Next, the Byxroids were given the necessary commands for the expansion project. All these hadn't been mentioned until then because they were considered a precautionary procedure. The Council was the center where all suggestions and ideas of commune people were discussed. The Council presented Ellie and Diane's suggestion to the commune people. The voting concluded with full participation as expected and the transportation to the bases was approved by everyone. New tasks were uploaded to the world production centers. The Byxroids at the production centers were removed from their work areas. They were recruited for a construction project at transitory bases in space and on the Moon where all living beings and their DNA samples could be preserved and protected.

First, all the important and historic assets were going to be temporarily transported to the bases on the Moon. Next, the data about all civilizations on Earth was going to be backed up at certain stations in outer space. And in four hours, the evacuation of 172,753 people living on Earth was going to be completed. The Commune Council was also concerned about the lives of people in other colonies living in isolated regions without communication. They had to be evacuated and separate bases had to be constructed for them as well. A notification was immediately sent to the people living in those colonies apart from the commune. They were going to determine their destiny either by following or not following the commune's decision. Finally, depending on time and housing capacity measures, almost all animals on Earth were going to be evacuated.

The Commune had downsized the risks to minimum by taking precautions for a probable worst scenario. The next step was to find out how to stop that object.

CHAPTER 15

Ben and Gabriel had reviewed the details on their way to the university. As soon as they arrived at the university building, they went into the room where HISD was available and got down to their history research.

They had mapped the observation area by aerial photography. They had specifically located the holy buildings where men used to gather at on Friday mornings to worship. They had been listening to the conversations in those temples as well. Ben and Gabriel were working separately on different locations. They were going to act together when they found something but their long search resulted in disappointment. They hadn't found anything, not even a single clue. No matter what, they continued their search attentively.

After some time, while Ben was scanning one of the areas, he noticed a young woman working in the courtyard of a temple. He began examining the temple; everything looked ordinary. After viewing the streets by the temple, he decided to go down to the village thinking nothing would come out of that temple. He was about to move on when he saw the young woman at the temple throwing up all of a sudden.

He had never witnessed anyone throwing up before. He found this very interesting. Therefore, he decided to stay in the area for a while to observe the young woman. Just then, she straightened up and found herself in a dust cloud the wind had blown up. However, Ben wanted to continue examining her. Nevertheless, he thought he shouldn't be hanging around there and wasting time. So, he decided to leave the scene to examine the rest of the village. But right at that moment, he noticed her looking at him carefully.

She was not only looking toward him but she was looking straight at him. They had almost made eye contact. Ben was surprised. The woman started to rub the dust on her eyes, then she looked straight at Ben again. The woman had seen him. But Ben had no idea how this could have been possible. How was that possible?

Soon after, she began murmuring something, her eyes closed. Then someone inside the temple called her name:

"Mary!"

So, this was her name, he thought. He felt uneasy thinking this could be a connection. This was a very common name in that region, so it could be a coincidence. He was preoccupied with those stories. He wondered if they were real or not. Once upon a time, a woman called Mary giving birth to a boy and naming him Eesho was possible. And this boy growing up, becoming an important leader, and being announced a prophet were possible as well. He was sure the story had been changed a lot in time. The name Eesho was changed to Jesus in 1684. Even if this young woman was that Mary, he might have a hint about ZA, who had leaped into their time somehow. He would finally make a big discovery that would uncover this myth. Besides that, he would have a chance to find the information to protect Earth and humanity from the upcoming danger.

He had to ignore his excitement for a while because Mary had seen him. At least he thought she did and he had to be sure about that. He wondered if she was looking at a spot behind him. Perhaps something in the tree he was standing near had attracted her attention.

He quickly went back to the moment he saw her and watched the scene again from a different angle. There was nothing interesting at the spot she was looking at. Now he was sure she was looking at him and she had seen him.

He informed Gabriel about what had happened right away.

"The woman's name is Mary, is that right?" asked Gabriel excitedly.

"Yes," said Ben. "The most interesting thing is she saw me. It is not possible to have an effect on the lives of others or to make contact with any living or non-living beings during these history travels we make. We are only observers; we can only watch what has been lived through. But that woman noticed me."

"How old was Mary?"

"I am not sure; she might be fifteen or even twenty. She must be in between."

"Take me there, to that moment," said Gabriel excitedly.

"Like I said, I can't take you anywhere in real terms. We can only make observation."

"Yes, yes, that's what I meant."

Ben let Gabriel watch the moments; the woman throwing up at the temple and seeing Ben. They watched the same scene over and over again from different angles.

"My God," said Gabriel., lifting his head up. Then he turned to Ben.

"We've found Eesho's mother, Ben," he said excitedly with a smile on his face.

"How can you be so sure it's her?"

"In those times women were not allowed in the temples. Mary's mom thought she was having a baby boy so she had devoted her child to the temple. And when Mary was a little girl, she was introduced to the temple by her aunt's husband. She had been educated and at the same time she had served God here. You can't come across a girl named Mary at any of the temples in this region. Therefore, I have no doubt about her identity. Just look at her, she's vomiting. She must be pregnant with Eesho.

Ben remained indifferent to his words.

"Oh sure, I always forget about your mutation. I meant physical pregnancy in women create some side effects like nausea and vomiting."

"Yes, sure," said Ben feeling annoyed for lacking this information on the subject despite being a historian.

"Do you think it is possible that she would see me, too?"

"I just don't know. What has happened recently makes me think everything is possible."

"Then I have a request," said Gabriel in a self-confident manner.

"If it's possible, I'd like to take a closer look at that temple. I want to watch the moment from the gate of the temple when they called Mary from inside."

"All right then, let's watch it from that angle."

"One more thing," said Gabriel. "I'd like to make an observation there alone for a few seconds. I'm aware that I won't be there physically, but mentally and spiritually I am here right now. I want to be alone at a place that is holy for me for only a few seconds. It won't take long."

"All right," said Ben.

The Believers had approved Ben having access to this blackened part of the history and this had happened with the help of Gabriel. He thought Gabriel deserved this privacy and respect.

After sending Gabriel to the gate of the temple, he continued his research on the same time period. He noticed that he had missed a detail while he was focusing on Mary only. He perceived a small area in the sky getting blurry continuously around 150 feet behind his image. Although he changed his position twice, that blurry section followed him and appeared exactly in the same place and at the same distance. Ben couldn't make sense out of this. There must have been a mistake somewhere. Maybe that's why Mary could see him. He thought he had to show this to Ellie later.

Meanwhile Gabriel was trying to enter the temple at the gate. But he couldn't see anything but a dark space. He still couldn't believe he was there. He was so excited that he didn't even notice Mary walking toward the temple entrance after her name was called.

They made eye contact as soon as Mary appeared behind one of the pillars at the gate.

"Mother Mary," said Gabriel at that moment, fascinated with her.

"You will bring God's Son Eesho into the world."

"Who are you?"

"I am Gabriel and-"

All of a sudden Gabriel felt the ground shaking. First the image of the temple and Mary started to wave and fade away. Soon after he felt he was being sucked into a vortex. Then he found himself in a pitch-black space. Later he was in the room where they had started their observations. The quake was going on and it was so severe that he had to hold onto one of the desks in order not to lose his balance.

Ben was also confused. He hadn't communicated with his PYXOM to give a return command.

CHAPTER 16

"How was your time travel?" asked Ellie looking at Ben and Gabriel.

"We were able to find a young woman named Mary. Gabriel believes she is the mother of ZA. Mary saw me and even Gabriel, too. Besides that, Gabriel had a little conversation with her. During my observations in some close areas the images lost their clarity. Perhaps that's why Mary could see and talk to us. This is like supporting your hypothesis "the universe is not perfect". There was some sort of a glitch."

"This is interesting. You interfered in history. This is a paradox. How can this be possible?" said Ellie and then added.

"If our universe is a simulation, there must be a flaw within it."

"Also, we experienced an earthquake without a warning and my virtual call ended all of a sudden. There hasn't been an announcement from the Council yet. I'll communicate with others and inform you if I find anything."

"OK, but there is one more thing," said Ellie.

Ben had noticed the hesitant expression on Ellie's face.

"Yes. I'm listening."

"We think the object is most probably a discovery or an alien invasion spacecraft. Another probability is this might be a settlement of unfinished business between ZA and the object in a transitive dimension in the past." Ellie looked at him in a way asking his opinion.

A negative expression appeared on Ben's face. He waited for some time not answering Ellie. The negativeness on his face had become clearer to attract Ellie's attention.

"What's wrong?" Ellie asked finally.

"First of all, I must say I don't presume this. On the other hand, there are some texts related to the moment of ZA's or Eesho's death. And there might be a couple of details supporting this probability in these old texts."

"Like what?" asked Ellie.

Ben had noticed Gabriel listening to him carefully and so he hesitated for a while. Then, he ignored him and continued with his words, directing his attention to Ellie.

"According to the resources when ZA was crucified-" When Ben noticed Ellie was looking at him in a strange way, he felt he needed to make an explanation. "This is one of the ways of ending one's life," he added.

"Some resources talk about his ascension after he was put to death. It might take days or even weeks to resolve ZA's real life and death. The graves of many famous people haven't been located throughout the history. I will evaluate the issue with Gabriel and see if we can find anything."

"We don't have that much time. You know that, Ben, right? ZZ is capable of using the space worms." She looked at the timer on her screen and added.

"We have less than twenty-six minutes. We must plan during the remaining time because it can enter another space worm at any moment."

Ellie was confused but she didn't have time to waste. She turned on the multi-research task mode on her PYXOM right away to receive the latest developments. This way she could receive the data about ZA and ZZ and continue her study on the cause of the previous earthquake at the same time.

The expected announcement came from the Council at last. The epicenter of the earthquake was about thirty-eight miles from the region. Its magnitude was 9.8 and it had lasted 54.2 seconds. The reason for not receiving a warning from the earthquake notification system was still unknown. The region was being examined and the reason for the system error was being investigated.

There were some interesting developments about ZZ as well. Although it was bad news that it had covered a four-hour distance in four minutes, this study had speeded up the progress of the discovery debots to reach ZZ. Finally, humanity had been able to reach the detailed view of the object. But they hadn't obtained any results from the scanning. The material the object was made of was still not determined. The spheres inside the object were changing in both shape and color; they sometimes stretched into ovals and sometimes to a cone-like shape. And there wasn't a pattern in their movements.

Another surprising information was the object was not generating a magnetic field, a signal, or radiation. And also, no wavelengths were found. It didn't leave behind any particles that carried its characteristics, either.

It was decided to collect samples from the object to be analyzed. This task was loaded to the discovery debots. Right after that they were immediately sent to the object. When they reached the target and landed on it, they tried to hold still on the spheres that formed the object. Unfortunately, they were unsuccessful with this because the spheres were unstable and their surface was slippery. The vacuums underneath the debots were activated. Even the vacuums couldn't enable them to stand still on the spheres.

Then the debots were given a command to change their position and lock their Lax laser drills to the determined drilling points without landing on it. The drilling points were surrounded by half-sphere transparent shields to collect the particles that were expected to come out during the drilling process. The goal was to collect at least a tiny particle to have it analyzed.

When the cutting tip of the laser drill started to rotate, suddenly all the colorful spheres turned white. The cutting tips were rotating for nothing. The analyze report said there wasn't even one single particle collected. Despite the debots' drills trying it over and over, the results didn't change; there wasn't even a scratch on the object.

Thereupon, the debots were given a command to activate their cell killer and shredder VS beams. But again, not a sample was collected from the object.

Finally, the debots were given a command to move away from the object. Somehow, they weren't able to move despite the command. The tip of the drill was stuck to the object. Therefore, the debots were told to release the cutting tip of the drill on top of the object and move away immediately. But before they were able to follow the command, the spheres suddenly became active. They started rotating downward and pulled the debots into the object rapidly. Although the debots were given full speed to escape, it was too late to save them. All were swallowed by the object before the eyes of humanity. Everyone watching this was in a shock and totally terrified.

All the incidents that started a couple of hours ago with the appearance of ZA were quite extraordinary. Any attempt to identify the object was a disappointment. Before humanity got over with one unexpected occurrence another one followed.

Everybody was focused on the object. They were trying to create theories about what that might be. Even the people who didn't have any knowledge or experience in the area were showing great effort. The specialist commissions formed of commune members from all around the universe were sending suggestions to the Council. Every suggestion was sent to all commune members in order to be evaluated in virtual discussion rooms.

At the end, it was decided to take the next step; the object had to be stopped before it reached the Earth. Destruction seemed to be the final solution to stop it since all the attempts to analyze it were unsuccessful. Some out of control devastating outcomes might have come up during destruction. Therefore, the first option was to try to change its flight route.

As a second stage, the machines held in reserve were activated. These machines sent out shockwaves. They got near the object and sent out shockwaves for fifteen seconds. The results were checked; the attempt was unsuccessful. These machines were loaded at full capacity and sent back. This time they sent out shockwaves from the opposite sides, the back and the front of ZZ for forty seconds at full capacity. The power of the last shockwaves sent out to ZZ was strong enough to remove a planet from its orbit with half the mass of the Moon. The mother ship and everything surrounding her had been in turbulence because of the recently sent shockwaves. The data was checked right away. It was negative; the object's flight route hadn't been changed even a bit and its speed had remained the same. As a result, the second attempt was also unsuccessful.

Upon the suggestions of the commissions, as a third stage, meteor light screen shields with mixro cell MCS composed of carbonsegirtin were activated. Twenty meteor light screen shields were placed next to each other in the flying path of the object. These light screen shields were capable of stopping meteors twenty-three times bigger than the object. These were the most powerful shields humanity possessed. These shields had to stop the object this time. The object was approaching the screen shield at high speed.

The huge light screen shields created a balloon and absorbed the object as soon as they came into contact with each other. The compounds in the heating units were activated. The heat inside the balloon increased rapidly. The temperature had risen to 1000 degrees F. But still no transformation was observed. The temperature reached to 2000 F and then to 2700 F. This was the highest level at which the heat units could perform. All the known materials and minerals in the universe should have been melted by then at that temperature. This was a method they used for destroying the meteors that created danger for Earth and for the destruction of space stations that had to be replaced. This object was more like something that didn't belong to this dimension.

A new command was given to the heat units in the shield to decrease the temperature to –459 degrees F. The temperature in the balloon shield started to drop down rapidly. The goal was to create a sudden heat drop to freeze and shatter the object. The temperature had almost decreased to 0 from 2700 F. There hadn't been any change in the data until the temperature hit 0.

"I'm observing activation at pressure indicators," said Ellie.

"Yes, the pressure is increasing," said Naochi.

"I don't see any reason for the increase in pressure at this intensity," said Ellie.

The temperature in the light screen shield had dropped down to –459 degrees F. The expected frozen state of the object hadn't been shaped. All of a sudden, the light screen shield began to swell and expand because it couldn't resist the pressure. As the expansion grew, cracks began to form. It wasn't able to stand the pressure any longer and finally exploded.

The power terminals that would provide power to the space stations were yet on their way and it didn't seem possible for them to reach the scene in time. There was only one solution left: to activate the Fusionuc units to attain high impulse.

Fusionuc units were kept idle at a distant colony from Earth. CME (Coronal Mass Ejection) was a form of energy and a plasm that appeared after the explosions in the Sun. The hydrogen and helium gases in this plasm were ionized by losing their electrons because of high heat. They also contained high radiation. Storing this energy and canalizing it was called Fusionuc, and because it consisted of nuclear power and high radiation, the usage of this technology was ceased after its first testing. Articles of the Constitution called Universe, Harmony, and Life that everyone had to follow prohibited the usage of this technology officially. This prohibition could only have been removed temporarily under certain circumstances. The prior condition for this to happen was, not only the whole planet but humanity had to be under threat. The next condition was the voting for the usage of nuclear energy. The voting required full participation and it had to be accepted with 95 percent of the votes.

Finally, the voting started and brought along a big discussion. Heated arguments had started in the commissions and on other platforms. Actually, almost everybody agreed this was against human values and principles. But while some were saying this had to be done for the future of Earth as a final solution, others were against falling back on this technology in any condition.

"How could this deadly war element be the fundamental structure of a peaceful society? Our planet might be under threat but humanity, all species on Earth, and even cultural heritage can be saved by being accommodated on spacebases. We should not fall back on this solution when we confront a threat," reacted some people. They were against passing on a shameful legacy like this one to next generations.

Some others said this planet was a heritage from ancestors and should be protected as much as the living beings were protected. In other words, they said the protection of the planet had to be a priority as well. "Our Earth, our home, our habitat, and all our memories will lose their physical reality; carrying them to a virtual environment doesn't mean saving them," they argued.

Another group of people claimed that other perfect worlds could be created.

On the other side, some were against the idea of creating an artificial world. "The same nature and the variety in it, the sun and other natural events cannot be created artificially," they said.

All of a sudden, humanity had found itself in a position to make a serious decision that would determine the planet's fate. They had to compromise on the issue. And this was a huge responsibility for all.

CHAPTER 17

When the time travel ended suddenly, Gabriel found himself in a vortex first and then in the classroom moving to and fro like a swing. He was alarmed. His extremely ordinary life had changed so fast in the last couple of hours. He had gotten confused and had almost lost his balance because of all those incidents that happened recently.

Gabriel had been mumbling something since he returned to the classroom.

"God save me from your wrath," he said.

The earthquake was still on. While he was trying to hold on to the table tightly, he thought he had the wrath of God upon him because he had made that history travel. He thought he shouldn't have been there in the first place. And he shouldn't have talked to Mary as well.

When the earthquake ended, he had taken out the cross on his chest and kissed it. Then he had got on his knees and started praying.

Gabriel had finally calmed down a little when Ellie called Ben.

"Is there a new development?" asked Gabriel to Ben when he ended his conversation with Ellie.

Incidents were proceeding at a fast pace and Ben was in such a state he didn't know which incident he had to focus on. Nevertheless, he put his thoughts in order and told Gabriel the latest news he had received from Ellie.

"I can't go on to another time travel. I would make a big mistake if I did that," said Gabriel. "From now on, I've left everything in God's hands."

"There are powerful earthquakes happening all over the world now," said Ben when he saw the data on his PYXOM.

"And there are tsunamis going on following them. None of these were predicted by our disaster detection system. Our defense systems should have stopped these quakes before they happened. But they didn't. A wild fire began in your colony land- the holy land. And there is an unidentified object approaching Earth at a fast speed. We can't just wait and do nothing. I'd better get back to my work."

"My friends have taken Eesho to the holy land. I must get there, too, right away. They might need me," said Gabriel and then turned his back to get ready for his journey.

"Is there any way of getting support or an idea from you to find the time and place of ZA's execution?" Ben called after Gabriel.

While Gabriel was getting onto his vehicle provided to him by the commune, he answered, "Even if you could travel to that moment, you won't be seeing anything but an execution scene. If you believe in God's mercy and his words that are beyond what you can see, then you can see Eesho 's ascension to Heaven through your heart"

Gabriel was speaking clearly and gently as if there was a five-year-old listening to him. Ben regarded this manner more like arrogance, not sincereness. It was as if Gabriel was pitying him. Ben was a poor human who had to be saved. That's what Gabriel was thinking. He also saw himself like a big-hearted person who would never give up trying to save Ben. His so-called understanding manner and his soft tone might have been a mask he had used unconsciously to hide his arrogance.

What disturbed Ben wasn't him uttering his beliefs. Gabriel trying to pull Ben to his side was disturbing him. He wanted Ben to put aside everything, count on his Eesho, and so-called God's signs. He wanted him to believe in those tales. In other words, he was trying to transform

Ben to himself. If he didn't do so, he believed Ben's soul would be in agony.

"All right," said Ben accepting the fact that he would be alone in this from now on. Definitely, he wasn't going to argue about that because he didn't have a reason to persuade Gabriel anyway.

Ben got back to his work after Gabriel left. He was following the developments at the same time. He found out that the earthquakes, wild fires, and tsunamis were followed by volcanic activities. These volcanoes had been inactive for centuries and now they had become active. He also found out that voting had started for using the Fusionuc power to change ZZ's route.

He was looking at the screen indecisively. The experience they had in time travel, their return, all these disasters on Earth and Gabriel's strange conversations… All these were too much for him. Besides these, he had to focus on the voting right now. But he needed a serene mind to make a decision on such an important matter.

"Ellie," he said to himself. She was the only one who could provide this serenity to him. "Have you found out the reason for these disasters? Do they have anything to do with that object?" asked Ben to Ellie.

"No, not from this distance. If it was closer to Earth, we would consider the object had an effect on water, fault lines, and even our systems by creating a strong gravitational force. But from this distance, any object of its size cannot have such an effect and gravitational force," said Ellie. Then she added after a short pause.

"I haven't established a theory yet, but all these disasters occur at remote areas, away from human settlements. Except the wild fire that is close to the colony of the believers and the earthquake in our colony."

"What does this mean?"

"The epicenter of the earthquake we had wasn't too far, but in other earthquakes there isn't even one colony in a thirty-mile radius. This radius is a lot more for the volcanic activities-at least 125 miles. It's the same for the tsunamis. There aren't any settlements at the shores they hit."

"I remember years ago the byxbots were programmed to organize the earth strata on the fault lines that formed earthquakes. They had stepped out of line and undertaken some other tasks they had created. Then the task was given to byxroids."

When Ben reminded her the byxbots, Ellie reflected on their working area, the fault lines on her screen.

"Can byxbots have a role in the formation of these 192 earthquakes the Earth has experienced recently? As you already know natural disasters don't act selectively."

"Then could there be a systemic conspiracy related to those natural events?"

"It seems like that for now. But this can change. There are commissions consisting of specialists of this subject. We can share this data with them and follow the later developments. If we keep digging into this subject right now, it might be a waste of time for us. The evacuations will begin in a couple of minutes."

"One last question. What do you think about the voting?"

"To me, it's an ethical decision. We have our Earth on one side and our principles on the other, so, to speak. I'm in between. What do you think?"

"Same. I'm in between. But I think I'll decide on Earth. For once, perhaps we can ignore our principles for a bigger purpose; for our planet. Then we can try to recover from the destruction we created,"

"Actually, we don't have a chance to choose. Even if the use of Fusionuc power is approved, we will choose that because we think we have to. What if it isn't like that in reality? What if our controlling instinct and the sense of power came with our evolution are provoking us to distort the facts? Wouldn't the next generations blame us for this?

"You are right. Our ancestors made the same mistakes by distorting the facts before the 70s photon belt period."

"Besides, the evacuation is about to begin. You should leave your studies aside and start getting ready. I will be in the last group leaving Earth. Many of the Believers are refusing to leave. The Council spokesperson Diane that provides the communication with their commune asked me to join her in the holy land to convince them and talk to them for the last time. And I accepted. Also, my assistant Naochi, Dr. Anne, and Kelly will be there voluntarily, but I must get Pearl first."

"I'll meet you there as soon as I get Marco," said Ben decisively.

"There is a wild fire there. If you come, you would put yourself in danger for no reason," said Ellie giving him a concerned look.

"I insist. Send me the coordinates and the time," said Ben despite there were so many things that kept his mind busy. He thought he had to be near Ellie instinctively.

CHAPTER 18

The voting had ended. The ninety-eight percent majority decided to use the nuclear power to change the object's route. When the believers received a positive response from the commune council to participate in voting, all of them voted "no". They didn't want to leave Earth under any circumstances.

After the voting ended, they decided to board children on the first evacuation spaceships. The children were going to be accompanied by adults by all means. And these adults would be their counselors who knew the children and their needs very well.

When the children were sent safely, the rest were going to leave the Earth. Besides that, there were commissions established. These commissions consisted of at least twenty specialists in ten big spaceships. They were formed from voluntary scientists who would analyze the effects on Earth and Moon after the collision. They would find solutions to the problems that might occur on the bases. Also, a limited number of byxroids were assigned to these commissions. These commissions started stationing observation units on Earth and around it immediately.

The preparations for another colony's evacuation had also started.

The evacuation had to be completed in less than twenty-eight minutes. Ellie, Naochi, Ben, and Diane had chosen to stay on Earth until the last-minute thinking they might help with something during the evacuation. The spaceships under Kelly's command were going to be sent to the holy land to evacuate the Believers.

While the first evacuation ships were getting ready to leave the Earth, the Fusionuc power units that weren't used for centuries had arrived at the region where the object was expected. The Fusionuc power units' checks had been completed. The rest of the spacecrafts and debots had been sent to secure locations.

The Fusionuc power units were positioned on the object's path and were timed to explode when the object reached the spot. There was also a radiation absorber unit placed on the same path. An explosion was planned to happen close to the front surface of the object. But it was going to have an impact on the side of it. The goal was to make a slight change in its route. At that distance, even a 0.01-degree deflection was going to be enough to reroute the object. As a result of that, the object would move away from Earth and it would be oriented further from the Solar system.

The countdown started. All humanity waited with hope and in fear.

The expected explosion took place finally and a huge impulse was created. The explosion hit the object right where it was intended. The measurements were made immediately and it was seen that there wasn't even a slight swerve in the object's route. The object hadn't been affected by the impulse at all. In addition to that, 99.95 percent of the released radiation was collected by the absorber, but the remaining 0.05 percent of the spread hadn't been prevented. Everybody was disappointed.

Then the object suddenly disappeared. Soon it was confirmed that it had entered a wormhole once again.

The object seemed to be reacting to humanity's attempts to stop it.

After a two-minute wait, the object appeared again accompanied by the brown alert. The countdown timer was showing less time remaining for the collusion than it was expected. The object had traveled a 24-hour distance in two minutes with the help of the wormhole. So, this meant there was only forty-nine minutes to the collusion. The odd thing was the impact angle of the object had changed. According to the previous simulation it was the spot where ZA had appeared, but now it was the holy land. The object was going to crash into the Believers' colony.

Although some of the evacuation ships hadn't arrived at the bases yet, everyone except Ellie and her companions who wanted to stay on Earth until the last minute and the Believers who refused to leave, had been able to get out of Earth's atmosphere in twenty-eight minutes. The next step was to evacuate the animals and to transfer the historical artifacts. This process was going to take twelve minutes according to the calculations of the byxroids.

In the meantime, the time they needed to swerve the object from its route was calculated. If they couldn't find a solution to that in forty-eight minutes, the collision was inevitable.

There was nothing else to do. Humanity was experiencing despair for the first time in centuries. The huge MEVs, mobile energy vacuum stations that were positioned at certain places in space earlier, had been activated. But according to the recent countdown, it was impossible for them to get to the object in forty-eight minutes. Everyone was waiting desperately. There was nothing else left to do but to watch the destruction of Earth.

How would they get used to their new lives? The ones on the evacuation ships were leaving Earth with looks of yearning crossing their faces. Everyone had lapsed into silence. They had to watch Earth's destruction before their eyes. How could they be prepared for this tragedy?

People who had stayed away from each other until then were coming together and getting close to one another instinctively. Their hands had begun touching other hands as if giving support to one another while they were looking at their home one last time.

CHAPTER 19

The evacuation of all people and living things in the commune had been completed. There were only Ellie, Ben, Naochi, Kelly, and Diane left behind from the commune. All had one purpose- to convince the Believers who refused to leave Earth.

Tens of evacuation ships led by Kelly took off from the commune and arrived at the Believers' land after a short flight. The wild fires in the region were still in progress. The rising smoke veiled the field of vision. The ships had difficulty finding a proper area to land. Some of them were lined up hovering and waiting their turns since there wasn't enough space for landing. A race against time had started. They had to evacuate the Believers and board them on the ships as soon as possible. But the flames had surrounded the 3550 Believers. They were making an extra effort to put out the fire.

Ellie's private small vehicle landed on the scene with her cat Pearl. Far ahead, she saw ZA who had got quite old and the small group gathered around him while she was getting off her vehicle. Gabriel, Nasir, and Avram were also in the group. She noticed Diane was talking to them passionately. When Diane saw Ellie approaching, she ended her conversation and headed toward Ellie quickly.

"It's not working, Ellie. They are so stubborn, I can't convince them. They don't want to leave here. I can't believe this. They know they are going to die and they don't care. I can't understand this," she said exhaustedly.

Meanwhile, Ben appeared behind them with Marco beside him.

"What's going on here, Ellie? Why hasn't the evacuation started yet?" asked Ben.

Diane moved toward the ships.

After a short silence, Ellie looked at Ben.

"We can't leave them behind. None of them."

"Well, of course we are not leaving anybody behind, Ellie"

"They don't want to leave here. I don't know how to convince them," said Ellie sounding upset. She had become extremely emotional again and this was out of the ordinary.

"I promise, we will transport them," said Ben, trying to make himself believe what he had just said. How could he make such a promise? He felt he got closer to Ellie much more. This was going to take him a while to get used to this.

Ellie looked deep into Ben's eyes. She trusted him. She knew he would keep his promise. She believed him with all her heart and mind. She hesitated to speak. Instead, she just nodded.

Just then Gabriel came near them. "I guess it's time to say good bye," he said.

"According to our PYXOMs we have less than thirteen minutes for evacuation."

"We are not going anywhere without you," said Ellie facing Gabriel. "Therefore, there won't be any farewells." Then she continued her words pointing at the smoke.

"Look around you. You are surrounded by flames. It's only a matter of time before the fire spreads here. Look at your friends; all of you are exhausted. You are not able to think clearly. ZA looks old and ill. Dr. Anne asked for your permission to examine him and begin his medical treatments before it was too late, but you didn't let him go or get his exams. ZA is a creature that belongs to Earth. Because of your beliefs you've got the wrong idea that ZA only belongs to you."

237

"For the first time in our history we asked your help for this fire. But you sent your ships here instead of sending the byxroids that would help us put out the fire."

"Don't do this, Gabe. You know that life is of the utmost importance for the commune. All byxroids were sent to save the living things so there isn't enough support to help you with the fire. We came here to save you, not your homes."

Gabriel interrupted Ellie's words. "There are hundreds of Believers staying here trying to save their homes. Do you know what 'home' means to us? It means our life, labor, family, children, our ancestors, and our memories. That's what it means. And if we lose them, there's no reason for us to live. We turn into nothing. If we are to die, we will die in our own land. You call him ZA but He is our holy Eesho. He is our Savior. You always interpreted him wrong. You can't comprehend the message of his arrival to Earth. All these incidents are related to Eesho. He came to Earth and this has to have a meaning. We can't go against God's will. In other words, his place is next to us."

"You really believe that ZA will stop all this," said Ellie in a soft tone. There was no use in sparking an argument. She had sensed Gabriel was overexcited.

"I am not saying he will stop all this. But what I am saying is whatever that thing approaching Earth is, it has to be related to Eesho," said Gabriel, this time in a calmer tone.

"This hypothesis is no use because the object is going to strike right here, this place," said Ben.

Ben thought about how he had started his day and the things that happened until the time ZA appeared. Everything was quite ordinary. But with his appearance their lives had changed and become out of order. Undreamt of things had started to happen one after another in a couple of hours. They had sunk into despair to use nuclear power, the most destructive, dangerous and dirty technology of humanity that hadn't been used for ages. Finally, they had to make a decision. Now they were leaving their planet and accommodating everyone at temporary bases until they built an artificial world with new habitats.

"We've come across with so many phenomena we thought were impossible to happen in couple of hours. Therefore, even the very extraordinary theories can seem likely to us. Everything can be possible. We have only nine minutes left for the evacuation. We must go now," said Ben.

"My friends," said Gabriel. "Even though you don't want to say good bye and even though I don't like saying that either, we have to do this. God speed. I hope everything in your new world will be fine. And..." he paused. Then he made eye contact with both.

"And thank you very much for everything you did," he added.

Then he turned to Ellie.

"Dear Ellie," said Gabriel. "You've always been special for me and you will always be. Besides everything, I thank you for your friendship."

Ellie looked at Gabriel as if she couldn't believe her ears. She didn't want to say good bye to him. She thought Ben was going to convince them to leave but he hadn't. Why wasn't he talking to him more convincingly? Why wasn't he stopping him? … She thought they weren't going to leave anybody behind.

"No, Gabe," Ellie said finally.

"This time I won't be mad at you for calling me Gabe," said Gabriel. He had a teasing smile on his face. Thereupon, Ellie smiled back to him involuntarily.

"Believe me, I am sorry, but it has to be this way. And who knows may be the Earth will survive and you come back. Good bye," said Gabriel. He turned and went back to the direction he came from, near Nasir and Avram.

Ben caught Ellie's eye. Right at that moment, Diane came and gave an inquisitive look at Ellie and Ben. Ellie closed her eyes and looked away. Then Diane understood that the answer was negative.

"We couldn't convince them," said Ben turning to Diane.

"All right then, why don't we take ZA to the ship and give him the necessary exams there?" asked Diane looking at Ellie.

"I don't think the Believers will let ZA go with us. As a commune, do we have an official procedure with them for such situations?" asked Ben to Diane.

"We have never experienced anything like this," said Diane.

"If we could just get him on the ship for his medical treatment-"

Ellie interrupted before he could finish his sentence.

"Wait a second. Why haven't I thought of this before? Well, of course," said Ellie. She hadn't said anything until then; she was just listening. After a thoughtful moment, she made a sharp turn and moved toward the group standing with ZA and Gabriel. She looked quite determined.

Ben and Diane followed Ellie not knowing what she was up to.

"Please listen to me," Ellie said loudly looking at the small group.

Ellie caught everyone's attention and then continued speaking looking into Gabriel's eyes.

"There's something important for you to know. According to the last development, the object's point of impact is here. I mean where ZA is standing now. And this means, there is a link between ZA and the object. Gabriel, you asked me to evaluate the events from your point of view. What if that object is actually approaching ZA, not Earth?" said Ellie and waited for a while not saying a word.

Then she gazed at Avram and Nasir and added.

"Do you understand what I mean?"

Gabriel had locked his eyes on Ellie while she was speaking. When she finished her words, he turned his back without a response and started a conversation with Avram and Nasir. Then they heard Nasir's voice.

"Friends, gather everybody! We are leaving. Yes, you heard me. We are leaving," he said decisively.

"Where?" asked some of the Believers.

"What's going on, Avram?"

"We will take Eesho to the object, instead of the object coming to him. By this we might have a chance to save our world and homes. Let everyone know this. Let's start boarding the ships," said Avram.

As soon as Avram finished his words, the Believers called all together.

"Yess!!!"

"Of course,"

"Oh God, thank you!" some screamed with joy. They still had hope.

For the first time in ages they had complied with the so-called nonbelievers' ideas. On the other hand, the people who were fighting against the wild fire were informed. In a short time, all the Believers gathered in the area and started boarding.

Gabriel looked at Ben and Ellie and smiled. Ellie and Ben smiled at each other, feeling good for saving the lives of the Believers.

"Naochi called. We don't have much time. We have only six minutes for the take off," said Ellie.

CHAPTER 20

Gabriel helped ZA while getting on his KRYXO since he had got quite old to do it by himself. With a command, The KRYXO lifted off a little and then transformed into an armchair. It grabbed ZA so that he wouldn't fall and then moved toward the ship. ZA's appearance had changed a lot; his hair and beard had turned grey and gotten very long. He had difficulty breathing. His hands and legs were trembling. His skin was covered with wrinkles and dark spots. His veins had become visible under his thin skin. He was gazing blankly into the distance.

Gabriel stopped and looked around after accompanying ZA to the ship. His eyes searched for Fanda, his Golden Retriever, but he couldn't see him. Fanda always stayed with Gabriel but now he wasn't around. He got out of the ship. He looked further away. Again, he couldn't see him.

"Fanda...Fandaaa...come here boy!" he called. He called him a couple of more times walking away from the ship. Still, Fanda was not around.

Where could he be? There was a short time until the take off. He was beginning to feel desperate. Then he heard Ben.

"If you like I can help you find Fanda."

"I'll be grateful."

Ben called his dog Marco, a Jack Russel Terrier breed.

"Find Fanda and bring him to the ship," he commanded Marco.

"Could you call Fanda one more time Gabriel?"

"Fandaaa..." called Gabriel.

"His scent is needed as well," said Ben.

"Fanda always stayed around me," said Gabriel.

Marco sniffed the bottom of Gabriel's robe and then looked at Ben.

"Run! Bring him here! You have five minutes."

Marco sprang as soon as he heard Ben and left the place. Pearl came right after him and then started running after Marco.

Fanda had never left his human before. He used to be with Gabriel all the time. But he was very hungry and for the first time his human had forgotten his feeding time. He had barked at Gabriel twice, trying to remind him, but Gabriel was too busy and pensive to see Fanda. Therefore, he had decided to take a chance at some other places to find food.

The smell coming from an empty barn had attracted him. He wasn't aware of the fire because he was too eager to find food and suppress his hunger. After he got inside the barn, a strong wind closed the barn door on him. As soon as the door closed, the flip latch outside the door fell into the catch plate and locked the barn door completely. Fanda was locked in the barn. When he heard the clicking noise, he looked up at the door. He saw that his exit had been closed. And when he turned back, he noticed the flames in the barn moving toward him. He panicked and started running around in the barn looking for an exit, but he couldn't. The only exit was the door the wind had closed and it was latched from the back. Once more, he tried to find another exit and keep away from the flames. He had forgotten how hungry he was. He was in trouble.

Then he heard his human's, Gabriel's voice. He was calling him. He was excited; he started barking so that he could hear him. He heard the unlocking sound of the flip latch on the other side of the door and then the door opened slightly. He was expecting to see Gabriel but instead he saw a dog and a cat staring at him. He was surprised. Those were Marco and Pearl. He quickly sprung over Marco and Pearl and got out of the barn. He looked around, expecting to see Gabriel but he wasn't there. Marco had imitated Gabriel's voice. Marco barked at Fanda to follow him. They started running toward the ship.

"Fandaaa…" called Gabriel's voice at his back.

Fanda had heard his human's voice again. He slowed down and then stopped for a second and looked back. Behind him, there was only Marco and Pearl running with him. His human was not there. Marco had been teasing him; he had imitated Gabriel's voice again. He was sure it was his human's voice. He paused and then watched Marco and Pearl running ahead of him. Marco gave Pearl a naughty smile while Fanda was watching them running. Then Pearl replied to Marco by imitating his barking. They were not real living pets but these two byxroid pets had played a joke on a real dog.

There was only one ship left on Earth. It was the ship that had ZA, a few Believers, Ellie and her friends on board. All living things and all necessary equipment had been sent to space with other ships. They were on their way to new bases. Meanwhile on the ship, the countdown had started for departure.

"Ten seconds to closing the doors," the announcement on the ship was heard. The captain of the ship, Kelly, had made the announcement.

Gabriel, Ellie and Ben were standing at the gate, looking forward to their pets returning.

When they were about to lose hope, Ellie pointed at the right side of the ship.

"Look!" she said.

When they all looked at where Ellie was pointing, they saw Marco, Pearl, and Fanda running at top speed toward the ship.

"Two seconds to closing the doors," announcement was heard.

First Fanda jumped in, right after him Marco, and finally Pearl. The doors closed and in no time the ship had took off. All three were taken to the quarantine and disinfected. The Earth had been abandoned entirely and its fate was sealed.

CHAPTER 21

The earthquakes had become more frequent in the last few minutes. These earthquakes were both closer to the region and a lot more severe. On top of that, in a few seconds the storm clouds had gathered in the sky and the ship was surrounded by tornadoes all of a sudden. As the ship was speeding up, invisible little marble bombs that turned air into space were sent out from the holes in front of it. When these marble bombs were fired routinely throughout the ship's route, this lowered the friction coefficient to zero that prevented the ship from gaining speed. And when the anti-gravity feature was enabled, the ship gained acceleration. After a short bumpy ride, the ship headed to space. Soon it was far away from Earth. Ellie was in the control room with the others. She had started watching the Earth on her light screen in sadness while they were moving away.

None of them had ever witnessed these types of natural events and disasters before. All the colors on Earth had turned to grey. Earth was almost like destroying itself before the object reached to it.

Nothing is going to be the same again. We will only be living the reflections of a reality. The new Earth we will build will never be the same as the real Earth we lived on. This is our only home. We are leaving our past behind. We are at the beginning of a long struggle. We have rough days, months or maybe years ahead of us. But humanity will overcome this, Ellie thought. Then she noticed something odd on her face; she touched it with her fingers. This was a tear drop trickling down her cheek. She was lost in her emotions. She couldn't explain why.

In the control room, Naochi looked at her light screen to review the recent developments. Others had turned their screens into transparent mode, so that they could see each other as well while following the developments. There was less than two minutes to ZZ colliding with the Earth. But she noticed the numbers on the countdown timer on her screen were not going down, they were going up. The duration of the time to the collision was not decreasing. On the contrary it was increasing.

"The object is slowing down," she said in surprise.

"How?" asked Ellie.

Ellie began checking the data excitedly.

"ZZ's speed was synchronized with the orbital velocity of Earth moving around the Sun," she said after a short silence.

"The object's speed was reduced proportionally when we left the Earth moving at top speed toward the object. It is also deviating from its route."

"So, it's not going to hit Earth?"

"Oh no, it seems its target hasn't changed. Although the deviation degree is very low, it is changing its route."

Everybody was following the new development. They didn't know how to react to this. All scientists had been busy with their calculations. The object was still slowing down and its deviation degree was increasing gradually.

"Despite all efforts, we couldn't succeed diverting the object's route. But now, it's rotating. I wonder what it is up to," said Naochi.

"It's following us," said Ellie.

"Yes," said Naochi looking at her screen. "It is actually following us."

"Not us, it is following ZA," interrupted Ben.

Diane, Naochi, Ben, Ellie, and Kelly sitting in a circle found themselves staring at each other behind their transparent light screens. All of them were thinking the same thing. Ben started the conversation.

"OK now, what are we going to do? Are we going to crash into the object without doing anything?"

"Although ZZ has slowed down, the impact severity will be very strong," said Kelly and added.

"One minute forty seconds to impact."

"We have to secure the Earth," said Diane.

"I suggest changing the ship's path" said Kelly.

"We can't go to the Moon any more. Where are we heading?" asked Ben.

"We can trail it behind us for some time. Maybe we can find a solution during that time," said Diane.

"For how long?" asked Ben.

"Or," said Kelly, "I can make a fast reverse maneuver right before the impact so that both of us would be on a parallel line next to one another."

"What is the percentage likelihood of this?" asked Ellie.

"The percentage would have been high under the normal circumstances. But in this situation, for the object's unexpected decisions, I can't say much," answered Kelly.

In the meantime, in the medical room, Dr. Anne was giving ZA a medical exam. Gabriel,

Nasir, and Avram were watching her curiously. Gabriel noticed Eesho moving his lips, trying to say something. He got closer to ZA to hear what he was saying. He heard him speaking in Aramaic, Eesho's mother tongue.

"They are calling me. They say it's time for me to go," ZA was saying.

"Who is calling you?"

"Them."

"Who are they?"

ZA gave a blank look at Gabriel without answering. He looked very exhausted.

I think I know the answer to my question, thought Gabriel.

He quickly connected to the control room.

"The Almighty Eesho wants to go to the object," he said.

After Ellie got their consent by making eye contact with everyone in the control room, she answered Gabriel.

"As a matter of fact, this is what we want," said Ellie.

"We have to separate ZA from the mother ship and minimize our risks," added Ellie looking at the people in the control room.

When Kelly heard Ellie, she took action right away. "Eighty seconds to the impact," she said.

"I need ten seconds to complete the medical scan," said Dr. Anne.

Space Patrol Craft is ready to leave," said Kelly.

Gabriel heard their conversation in the control room and he exclaimed.

"I can't let The Almighty Eesho go by himself!"

"SEVENTY SECONDS TO IMPACT"

The countdown had begun automatically by the system. The ship's illumination turned into yellow and then to red.

"The Space Patrol Craft is only for two people," said Kelly.

"I am together with The Almighty Eesho," said Gabriel in a decisive tone. The Believers waiting behind Gabriel were quiet.

Another announcement was heard.

"SIXTY SECONDS TO IMPACT"
The ship's illumination turned brown.

While ZA was moving in his KRYXO armchair toward the Space Patrol Craft, Gabriel escorted him followed by the prayers of the Believers. When they reached the vehicle, first ZA went inside. Before Gabriel stepped into the vehicle, he turned around and looked at his fellow Believers.

"Goodbye, my friends," he said and then despite his age he got inside the vehicle in a swift manner. The door closed.

"The departure process is complete," said Kelly and gave permission to depart.

But there was something wrong; the Space Patrol Craft was unable to depart from the mother ship.

"10 SECONDS TO IMPACT"

The brown lights started flashing right after the announcement.

"The departure is not occurring," said Kelly trying to keep calm.

"As a last move I am getting the ship ready for a fast reverse maneuver, positioning us parallel to ZZ right before the impact," she added. Her rapid moves on the light screen weren't giving results. She repeated the same procedure a couple of more times but nothing had changed. Traces of panic and fear could be seen on her expression. Against all her efforts, she was not able to proceed with her plan.

"The ship is not responding to any of the commands. Get ready for the impact!" she exclaimed.

A smile had appeared on Gabriel's face. He had lived his life on a path he knew was right. Death was not an end or something to be afraid of according to his philosophy of life. On the contrary, death was the beginning. He was happy and tranquil. Knowing that he was going to heaven, he held Eesho's hand, closed his eyes and said his prayers quietly.

"EIGHT SECONDS TO THE IMPACT"

There was complete silence on the ship. No one was speaking; they were frozen with fear. A chaotic uncertainty was waiting for them and they had no time to make plans or to follow them. They were drawn into an unknown vortex helplessly. They were not ready for this. Moments ago, they had seen Gabriel smiling and his tranquil glance on their light screens but they couldn't make sense of it. He knew he was going to die but he seemed ready for it somehow. They were confused. All that knowledge, their discoveries, the technology they had developed, and their efforts to keep up Universe, Harmony and Life were all about to come to an end. They had always decided for their future. Then what was happening?

"SIX SECONDS TO IMPACT"

While these thoughts were running in their heads, Ellie felt a strange warmness in her hand. When she looked at it, she saw Ben holding her hand. She was filled with peace. She felt a sensation of warmth she had never felt before.

"FOUR SECONDS TO IMPACT"

Without hesitation, Ellie held Naochi's hand sitting next to her. When they saw them, Diane and Kelly held hands as well. Then others followed and joined the circle. The uneasiness that had grown within them was replaced by peace.

"THREE SECONDS TO IMPACT"

Everybody looked at each other for the last time. When Ellie closed her eyes, others followed her. In that short span of time, their lives flashed before their eyes. In the last third second Ben had felt weird. When he closed his eyes, he had seen an image of a huge male figure almost ten feet tall with long curly grey hair at shoulder length. He had a gray beard in layers making a triangular shape down to his chest. The dress he was wearing was in layers and touching the ground. His dress was the same color as his beard and hair. This man was glaring at him. Who could this be? he thought. He couldn't make sense of what he saw. Then he gave up. The end was near after all.

When Ellie closed her eyes, she saw two babies sleeping on her lap. She felt so much peace and happiness. But then she thought she would never have a chance to see them in life. She had come to an end. Their lives were about to end. However, she had a lot to do, a lot to achieve in her future. The subject "death" that she had been working on, thinking about and had taken most of her time was coming to her insidiously. And it was about to sweep away all her accomplishments without her consent.

The announcement was heard.

"TWO SECONDS TO IMPACT"

Their eyes closed; everybody was waiting for the impact.

Ellie couldn't figure out how time had slowed down while squeezing the hands of Naochi and Ben unintentionally. Then she started counting down.

"ONE…"

"Come on, strike!" Ellie screamed as if she was emptying the energy accumulated inside her.

"…ZERO!" said Ellie. "Good bye!"

CHAPTER 22

The illumination on the ship turned back to normal after the brown lights stopped flashing. Right after that an announcement was heard.

"NO IMPACT!"

Everybody was experiencing another big shock. It was as if they were paralyzed in their seats. Their hearts were racing. Their eyes were still closed. They were motionless and still waiting. Then all of a sudden Ellie and others felt pain in their hands. They had squeezed their hands so hard during the countdown that now their hands hurt. Kelly was the first to pull herself together. She had managed to get back to her light screen to analyze the situation as soon as she heard the announcement.

"We stopped before the impact," said Kelly. Then she transformed the external walls of the ship into transparent walls.

Shortly after that, others opened their eyes one by one and started moving slowly. But no one said a word; they were rendered speechless by the view they saw. The enormous object was floating there in space, radiating colorful lights before them at about 600 feet from their ship.

"The object happened to stop just before the impact," said Diane in an amazed manner. Gabriel and ZA had got out of the craft and entered the control room. Everyone was looking at ZA. He looked a lot older than before. They had never seen a person with so many wrinkles before. His head was shaking from left to right and his hands were trembling. These involuntary muscle movements in an uncontrollable and unintended way had attracted everyone's attention in the room. If his KRYXO hadn't covered his body in an armchair form, he wouldn't have been able to stand up in balance in such state.

Everyone was looking at him in astonishment and they couldn't find a way to support him. No matter how much they tried they hadn't been able to prevent him from aging. His bone structure had gotten thinner and smaller. And now he was helpless like a baby.

Just then, Dr. Anne entered the control room.

"How is ZA doing?" asked Ellie to Dr. Anne.

"He has twenty minutes left to live," said Dr. Anne.

"How is that possible?" asked Ben.

"As a result of his medical scan; he has cardiac insufficiency related to his old age, hypertension, and he has left main coronary artery disease. There's Alzheimer disease in his brain and in addition to that when we go down, he has colon and prostate cancers. Influenza pneumonia develops mostly in cardiac patients who have congestion in their lungs and causes death. I am not mentioning the other minor diseases. His aging gene code has been changed," said Dr. Anne.

"We can cure ZA and postpone his death, right doctor?" asked Ellie.

Dr. Anne reviewed the data on her screen.

"For an ultimate cure, mutation method should be applied and we need 4 hours for this process. The ones that require urgent treatment are cardiac and hypertension and these treatments only take 12 minutes. ZA has 19 minutes to live. I am not even mentioning changing the gene codes. Namely, it is impossible to change or stop his death from now on. Besides I am not taking into consideration other infections and their applications that might come up during this period. If we had a chance to step in earlier, the situation would have been different," said Dr. Anne.

Everybody was focused on her words.

Diane turned around and looked at Gabriel, who was making an evaluation of the situation with Nasir and Avram.

"We shouldn't have given ZA to them, Ellie," said Diane

"We trusted them about ZA and gave them a chance. As a Council we did not leave you alone in a situation that you seemed to be right about. But somehow, they got ZA under their control and they blocked rational decision-making mechanisms for this subject," said Diane

"You are right. The protocol between us and the Believers should have been more accurate about the options we had presented them," said Ellie and continued.

"We found ourselves on the same ship with ZA without questioning the reasons and before making the calculations of risks that might have occurred." Before Ellie finished, Dr. Anne interrupted, looking at her screen.

"Time is running out; 18 minutes to ZA's death."

"We don't have time for such conversation. What are we doing next?" asked Ben. He had been quiet most of the time but he felt he had to intervene.

Ellie knew the reason why she had accepted Diane's invitation to be on the same ship with

ZA and she hadn't shared this with her. One of the reasons she was on this ship was a little girl. How could she have explained this to Diane?

When she was on her way to pick up Pearl, the evacuation ship that was boarding children had attracted her attention. When she looked closely, she had seen Kate, the director of kindergarten, talking to a little girl. The little girl had noticed Ellie's vehicle and turned her head to look at her. This was little Emily beamed with joy, the girl who had invited her to play. But her brilliant joyful smile had gone. She looked very unhappy instead. She had gazed at Ellie hopelessly. Ellie had felt her unhappiness deep in her heart. She would have done anything to make her happy and smile again. I wish, she thought.

"The Almighty Eesho told me he wanted to go to the object," said Gabriel turning to the group.

"If ZA dies here, we might come face to face with an unpredictable danger again. In my opinion, we should transfer ZA to ZZ before he dies," said Ellie.

The pessimistic mood on the ship and the trauma they had experienced moments ago had been replaced by a stir back again.

"Let's send ZA on a different spacecraft or... we can go leaving him here on this ship," suggested Diane.

"Not only the two-passenger patrol vehicle but none of the spacecrafts can leave the mothership. There is a system lockup," said Kelly.

"How about the exits to outer space?" asked Ellie.

"They are still active," answered Kelly after checking it on her light screen.

"We can send ZA to ZZ with an UGISSI. This seems to be the only alternative," said Ellie.

Everybody in the room exchanged looks. Since there wasn't anyone coming up with a different idea, Ellie's suggestion was confirmed.

"OK, but sending him to space all by himself might put the Almighty Eesho in danger," said Gabriel.

"Please, I remind you that all humanity and Earth is in danger," said Diane in a reproachful manner.

Gabriel pretended he didn't hear what Diane had said.

"I'm going with him," said Gabriel decisively.

"Why?" asked Ellie; this didn't make any sense to her.

"The Almighty Eesho wants me beside him."

"But you have never wandered into outer space with an UGISSI,"

"I'll learn."

"You need a one-hour training to learn that. I am coming with you," said Ellie.

"If somebody has to go with them, I'll go," said Ben.

Ellie looked at Ben with admiration. Then she asked, "Why you?"

"Because you are striving for the future and the unknown. But me, I am at peace with the past and the common. There is more need for you here."

"But you-"

"All right, I got it" said Gabriel before Ellie finished her words.

"We really have to have someone going with us. I thank you both, but time is running out," he said impatiently. After looking at Eesho beside him worryingly, he turned to Ellie and Ben.

"Now please do what I say without an objection. Ellie, put your hand behind you so that Ben can't see it. I want you to make a one or a two using your fingers. And Ben will guess which number you are signaling. If he gets it right, he is coming with us and if he gets it wrong, you are coming with us. Is that a deal?"

Ben nodded showing his acceptance of the deal.

"But," Ellie said "I don't understand," showing her disapproval in a way. "I am the person who has to make the sacrifice," she added.

"You don't need to understand, Ellie. It's time to leave some things in God's hands," said Gabriel. This time his tone was more decisive and insistent. Gabriel felt like he was carrying the ball among the commune members.

The commune members stared at Gabriel, not knowing what to make of his words. Gabriel directing the events insistently and giving them an ultimatum were annoying the commune members but they didn't have time to argue this.

Gabriel looked Ellie in the eye wanting her to compromise. Ellie was not happy at all with the situation she was put in. She was uneasy because she felt Gabriel was taking advantage of her and he was using the concept of God ever since ZA was the subject. But at that moment there weren't any other options to choose from. She took a deep breath facing Ben. Then she turned her back to Gabriel and stood still. She put her hand behind where only Gabriel could see and signaled number two using her fingers.

"Two," said Ben after looking around the room for a couple of seconds.

In this case, Ben was going with Gabriel and ZA. Ellie looked displeased by this.

"We have to take the Almighty Eesho to the object as soon as possible," said Gabriel.

"Every second, he is getting closer to death. If he dies before he gets there, this might put us in danger," said Ben.

Kelly commanded the byxroids to prepare the three for their spacewalk.

Without wasting time Gabriel turned back to say his farewells to his fellow Believers. They said good bye to Gabriel and touched ZA for the last time.

"Don't worry," said Ben noticing the worry in Ellie's eyes. "Everything will be fine."

"I hope so," said Ellie trying to stay calm. She had noticed how Ben was trying to comfort her most of the time. Then she looked at Gabriel; all he cared about was his Eesho. She always observed events and human behaviors unbiasedly. But this time it was hard to accept this situation. Before he left the room, Gabriel hadn't said a word to her, not even a goodbye.

In the space exit room, after Gabriel and ZA took off their clothes, the GISSIs provided for Gabriel and ZA came out of KRYXOs and covered every inch of their bodies except their faces. All three got off their KRYXOs and stepped on the platform in front of them.

Ben opened his arms wide. Looking at Ben, Gabriel and ZA imitated him; they lifted their arms making a 90-degree angle. A beam of light scanned their bodies from head to toe and made measurements. Then their feet left the platform and they were suspended in air about two inches high. The panels from the back and front joined capturing their bodies inside the templates. These templates reopened after a few seconds. UGISSIs had been fit onto their bodies.

There were routers behind their ankles that looked like little fins. The eye part was made of a transparent elastic surface and this was the only organ that could be perceived. They could see outside from there and it also functioned as a screen. Although this elastic coating covered their bodies tightly, it didn't touch their faces. There was a quarter of an inch space between their skin and the coating. Also, in front of their nostrils and mouths there were small outward curves that had filters in them. These were the functional mechanisms that changed arraq particles into oxygen.

"There are routers on your ankles that will sense your movements," said Ben to Gabriel.

"You need to move your foot slightly to the direction you want to go. Keep in mind that they are very sensitive; you make sure you move your foot slightly. And also, you'll have sharper turns if your foot moves wider. Our speed will be controlled by the outfit automatically. If you wish to stop for any reason, verbal command will be sufficient. If you command to slow down, your speed will decrease gradually. If you say "Stop", you will stop right away. The sensors on the UGISSI will slow us down when we get close to the object. It is not possible for us to drift or bump into anything.

While Gabriel was listening to Ben's directions carefully, ZA was looking around unconsciously not knowing what was happening or about to happen. Hearing his own breath had scared him. He looked around slowly. Everyone and everything looked different. Then he saw the strange substance on his arms. He moved his fingers slowly. He was highly surprised but he was unable to give any kind of reaction related to his illnesses. He had so many questions in his head but he didn't know how to ask. Even if he asked, he didn't think he would understand the answers and therefore he preferred to keep quiet. He was feeling too exhausted to speak anyway.

"Everybody please leave the room and get behind the light screen," said Kelly.

Ellie moved ahead inside the ship and stood behind Naochi and Diane, who were standing in front of the window. They all started watching outside through the transparent exterior walls.

Diane placed her index finger on her middle finger. She had done this using her both hands.

"What is this?" asked Naochi. This hand gesture had attracted her attention.

"This is an old-time ritual for bringing luck," said Diane.

"I don't mind luck being on our side," said Naochi smiling. She imitated Diane and crossed her fingers like her.

Although their backs were facing Ellie, she could follow their hand gestures through the reflections on the ship's transparent walls. Her grandmother used to do that, too. This had a name...What was it? she thought. "Yes sure, this is superstition," she said to herself after a while.

Meanwhile, Kelly had been busy checking the recent situation of the object, making calculations on her light screen in order to find out if the particles in the region would provide enough oxygen or not. The countdown timer wasn't on the screen any longer. The particles in the region were sufficient. On their route there weren't any big meteor pieces that would cause an impact and harm them. But just in case, a light screen shield was going to be placed around the ship against the small meteors moving along at high speeds in outer space.

Meanwhile, Ellie's eyes had caught Diane standing there her back turned to Ellie. She carefully looked at the reflection of Diane on the glass window facing the outer space. The image of her fingers was reflecting on the transparent wall. She looked more carefully this time. Wasn't Ben standing where she was standing now while they were trying to decide who would go? When she was signaling number two behind her, she was standing at the spot where Diane was standing now. When she moved a little to the left, the reflection on the wall disappeared.

In order to be sure, she moved back to her previous spot and the reflection appeared again. Yes, this is the spot where Ben was standing, she thought. She recalled and imagined the scene. Ben actually had looked at the transparent wall while he seemed to be looking around. And he had done this on purpose.

"Conditions are positive," said Kelly, interrupting Ellie's thoughts.

"Are you ready?" asked Ben to Gabriel in the space exit room.

"Yes," said Gabriel.

"Door open," called Ben.

The metallic colored walls of the exit room suddenly disappeared and they found themselves in outer space. The object they called ZZ was standing right before them in all its grandeur.

As soon as their bodies fell into space, ZA looked for ground to stand on and when he couldn't find it, he began fluttering like a bird fallen into water. When Ben and Gabriel noticed him panicking, they held him tightly on both sides. ZA looked at Gabriel in fear, but trying to assure confidence in him, Gabriel smiled and pointed at the object.

Ellie got closer to the window with the excitement of figuring out Ben's trick. It was too late. All three were floating in outer space now.

"Why?" asked Ellie as soon as she had intercom with Ben.

"Why what?" asked back Ben.

"I know about your little trick. But why?"

"I respect you Ellie. I couldn't have put you into risk," said Ben in a calm manner.

"Could you look over here?"

Ben turned his head to Ellie, his eyes zooming in of the control room.

Ellie made a big heart on her light screen. Inside the heart, on one half she drew a blue male symbol and a pink female symbol on the other half of the big heart. Then she looked at Ben.

When Ben realized Ellie wanted twins, he smiled and right at that moment he let go of Gabriel's hand for a second and made two thumbs up showing her he was okay with that decision. Then he quickly turned and held Gabriel's hand again.

Upon this, she smiled back and she murmured while she was making a two using her both index fingers.

"A girl and a boy. Yes. Everything will be great." She was trying to have hope for her future.

CHAPTER 23

When Ben, Gabriel and ZA reached the object it had stopped its movements completely. The spheres had turned white and they were motionless. The whole commune held its breath. They were watching the three men through their PYXOMs anxiously. Dr. Anne was following ZA's medical condition through the data coming from his UGISSI. There were 6 minutes left to ZA's death.

Ben directed Gabriel and ZA toward the object while holding their hands. When they reached the top of it, he signaled Gabriel for landing and they started to descend. At that moment the micro vacuums appeared underneath their feet to complete their landing by attaching to the object.

However, they were not able to complete the landing.

"What happened? What's the problem?" asked Ellie when she saw them stopping at about ten feet to the surface and floating in space.

"I don't know," said Ben. "We are so close to the surface but we can't contact it."

Ellie checked if the routers of the UGISSIs were functioning well. Then she turned to Kelly.

"Are the shields active?" she asked.

"Negative," answered Kelly.

"There doesn't seem to be a problem," said Ellie to Ben.

Ben and Gabriel tried to land one more time after Ellie's response. But they couldn't succeed.

"It's like the object is pushing us back- "

"We are trying to figure out what's happening," said Ellie. She looked away from her screen and turned her head toward the object, hoping to detect something while she zoomed in on the object using her naked eye.

"Everything looks normal," she added.

Right after she said that, she noticed a movement in ZZ. The spheres that formed the object were changing color rapidly.

"The object is vibrating. Something is wrong!" said Ben.

"I am analyzing this right now," said Ellie. Others also reviewed the data on the screen in order to understand what was happening. Before they had any results from the analysis, they saw the spheres changing colors and rotating slowly among themselves.

All except ZA, who looked extremely exhausted, were in great surprise. Gabriel was worried, but seeing ZA's serenity comforted him. Instead of trying to figure out the things going on around and react to them, he preferred leaving it in God's hands.

Ellie was doing her best to figure out what was going on. Although she could observe the vibration of the object, the scanners couldn't obtain new data from it. Despite what she saw, the data didn't indicate any change at all. It was as if the object was playing a game on them. What she had witnessed with her naked eye wasn't matching with high technology scanners' data.

"Ellie, look at that," said Naochi suddenly.

"Ellie looked at the image Naochi had sent. The sizes of ZZ and the three men were differing continuously depending on time and distance factors.

"I don't understand," said Ellie after reviewing the images and the numbers on her screen.

"Look at the distance between us and ZZ. Neither the object's nor the spheres' sizes change when the three move toward the object. But the images of the three are shrinking when they get closer to the object."

"What's wrong with that?" asked Ellie.

"Everything looks normal until you see this. Now look closely. This is the moment they couldn't land on the object. Despite the fact that their speed is zero compared to the object at that moment, their images shrink every second."

She continued after zooming in on the image of the three shadows falling upon the object.

"The shadows change place. If the speed of the three was zero compared to the object, then their shadows had to be stable. But the size of ZZ and the spheres forming it look the same from this perspective. Isn't this odd?" she said and looked at Ellie.

"As a result…"

Naochi showed the image of ellipse shaped object from sideways and then its current image.

Ellie looked at both images of the object from sideways. There was an evident structural difference between the two images. When it was seen from the front view there wasn't a difference. But when it was observed from sideways, its previous structure looked different. The current image of the object was expanding backward and turning into a pit that looked like a bowl-shaped object. It was getting more and more deep and transforming into an elliptic cylinder.

"This object is definitely playing a game with us. It is causing an illusion; although the spheres are expanding backward and getting bigger, you don't see the change when you take a look at the front view of the object. But the sizes of the three are shrinking every second they are moving away from us," said Naochi.

"Leave the object right away!" Ellie exclaimed as soon as she realized what was going on.

"Right now!"

Ben and Gabriel tried to ascend by lifting their toes slightly. However, the object they were trying to land on moments ago was not letting them go now. While looking around hastily, they noticed the spheres inside the object were folding on top of each other and rising up like a wall and surrounding them. They were too late to find out that ZZ was playing a game on them. Hadn't ZZ got its name from a game called "puzzle" anyway?

"Ben, Gabriel! Get away from that now! It's swallowing you!" exclaimed Ellie once again.

"We can't!" said Ben.

"ZZ doesn't let us go. I sense some sort of gravitational force."

While the sphere wall was surrounding them, their space view had begun to become narrower as the walls became taller. Ben, Gabriel and ZA had found themselves in a structure that was in the shape of a cylinder.

Gabriel turned and looked at Ben. Although he had traces of fear and panic on his face, he looked as if he was trying to be in control.

"This is God's will," said Gabriel finally.

"God chose us for this important mission. He will show us mercy."

Gabriel was ready to accept the things as they were.

Ellie, who was watching the developments turned her back.

"No! No! No!" said Ellie her voice trembling.

"Diane...Naochi, there must be something we can do. We must be doing something wrong."

"We did everything we could," said Diane. She sounded exhausted.

"I am so sorry," said Naochi lowering her head.

"Kelly, let's send a rescue vehicle," said Ellie.

"I'm trying, but it doesn't work," answered Kelly in a hopeless tone.

Ellie turned around and saw Avram and Nasir praying, their eyes closed.

"You've been praying to your God. I am asking you, then why doesn't your God stop this nonsense?" She sounded like she was complaining. She realized she wasn't able to control her feelings anymore and she didn't really care.

"They are appearing before God. I wish we had a chance to reach that level as well," said Nasir.

"This could be fine with ZA and Gabe, but what about Ben?"

"I am sure he will also be secure before God. Patience is a virtue. We must show patience," said Nasir.

"How come I don't feel that security for them?" asked Ellie.

Nasir took a deep breath. He knew it wasn't the time or place for this debate, but the gauntlet had been thrown down.

"Dear Ellie, for us, God is the infinite greatness but you call God as "The Harmony of Universe". We trust God unconditionally and we are trying to lead His way without questioning. And you say universe is in harmony with life, but you couldn't trust the universe even once. You couldn't even change one of its principles. It's not up to me but it would be better if you add "Trust" to the trio of Universe, Harmony and Life in your constitution. After this minute, the only thing we can do is to show obedience to God, accept what He has planned for us and wait patiently," said Nasir.

Ellie was not prepared for this. She wasn't in the mood for a debate and also, she didn't have time for that. She didn't have anything on her mind. She was confused. Her closest friends were slipping through her fingers.

"I don't feel like talking about this," she said and turned her back to Nasir and Avram.

For her, desperation was the stage where options and probabilities were at an end. This situation had put her in the stage of desperation and this had brought rage along.

The most valuable two people in her life were vanishing before her eyes. She leaned both hands on the transparent wall and her eyes zoomed in on Gabriel and Ben who were about to disappear into the object.

She saw Ben looking at her from the closing gap. The intercom was on. They could still hear each other. He smiled at her.

"Will you name the baby boy Burke?" he asked.

These words hardly came out of his mouth. They were Ben's last words just before his journey to the unknown.

All he cared about was not seeing Ellie again and not having the children they had dreamt of. These thoughts were a burden for him emotionally. The only thing he could console himself with was he was there instead of Ellie.

"Goodbye, Ellie," he said finally while the walls around him were getting higher.

Ellie looked at Gabriel. His eyes were closed and he was holding ZA's hand tight. He seemed to be praying,

"Ben! Gabe! I'm so-"

Before she could finish, the spheres around the object rose suddenly, closed over their heads and swallowed them.

CHAPTER 24

The communication was interrupted. The conversation traffic on the PYXOMs had stopped and everybody was quiet. This alien object had swallowed them before their very eyes. Except the color changing, there was no other movement in the object. It was right there floating in space magnificently.

Ben and Gabriel were also confused and shocked like the people who were watching them on their screens. They were not dead. They couldn't be. Besides, their conscious was telling them they were alive. They were inside the object now but they had no idea what it was. Inside was pitch black and they were waiting and holding hands tightly not knowing what to do.

Then they felt something like an ivy climbing up from their feet. In fear, they tried to touch it using their free hands to find out what this thing was. Whatever this was, it was moving along inside their GISSIs and they were not able to touch it. They could not perceive anything but their UGISSIs.

Ben finally pulled himself together and turned on the light source switch on the arm of his UGISSI. Then Gabriel did the same. But the only thing they could see was darkness and they were floating in it. Although they felt the presence of something inside their bodies, they couldn't see it.

"Something is happening. It's like something is wrapping my body," said Gabriel to Ben.

When he didn't have a response from Ben, he turned and looked at him. He only saw Ben's eyes staring at him in surprise.

The communication link between us must have been interrupted, Gabriel thought.

Then before they knew, they were sucked up by a huge force. All three were dispersed in different directions. ZA had slipped from their grasp. Even though they tried to grab him, they were not successful. Then they felt all their energy being sucked up.

Gabriel was about to pass out. While ZA was moving away, the spheres between ZA and

Gabriel were building a wall around him and radiating brightly at the same time. He could still see ZA. Ben was floating a little further from him. He pointed his light to Ben and looked. There wasn't any sign of movement and his eyes were closed. Then he noticed the spheres rising like a wall between them. The object was separating them from each other and building a wall around them. He turned his head hoping to see ZA while the spheres were closing over him. They gave off bright light. Then he saw ZA being dragged deep down into the gigantic object. Right behind ZA, a gleaming item in the shape of a chest caught his eye.

Seeing that chest had made him forget about Ben and ZA for a while. He forced himself to stay awake, trying not to close his eyes so that he could be certain of what he was seeing. He wasn't able to see or think clearly any more. But he was able to say, "This is the Ark of the Covenant!" Then he could no longer resist; his eyes closed. He passed out.

When he opened his eyes, he found himself drifting away in outer space. He looked around him and the first thing he saw was the object. Then he tried to remember what had happened. Everything had happened so fast. He began remembering. The object had swallowed them, then it had let them go out, back to the outer space.

He noticed Ben passing by him floating; his legs and arms open. But Ben's condition seemed different to him.

"Ben!" he called loudly.

But he couldn't get a response from him. He tried to reach and grab him, but he couldn't. He had tried to use his UGISSI but he was so excited that he had given a reverse command; instead of going forward he had gone backward. He wasn't able to think properly. He was confused. However, he remembered ZA all of a sudden.

He wondered if the object had let ZA go back in outer space too.

"Ben! Gabe! Can you hear me?" Gabriel heard Ellie calling. But he was too exhausted to answer her. While he was forcing himself to stay awake and go after Ben, he couldn't help looking at the gleaming object.

"Gabe!"

He heard Ellie again.

Then all the voices stopped and all the colors turned to black.

CHAPTER 25

The object had closed up again after throwing Ben and Gabriel out. Their communication with ZA had been broken completely and the object had begun shrinking. But Ellie was not taking into consideration the data coming from the object because Ben and Gabriel's bodies were drifting to a region where meteor rains were very common. She had paid attention to the data coming from the region.

Drill, patrol, and other spacecraft were no longer disabled. They could leave the mother ship any moment. As a first thing, the vehicles had been sent with byxroids in them. Their task was to bring Ben and Gabriel back to the ship. They reached them finally and after a short quarantine process, they were transferred to the vehicle safely. The mother ship was notified that they would be back in twenty-three seconds.

They were both unconscious but their vital signs were stable.

Dr. Anne asked through the intercom,

"Do you see the data Ellie?"

"Yes, it seems they are in good health," said Ellie.

"Do you have any idea about Gabriel's age?"

"We are the same age. I mean 150."

After a short pause Dr. Anne continued;

"Gabriel's present anatomic age is thirty-six."

"But how is that possible?"

While Ellie was reviewing the new data, she was watching the images coming from the scanners. She didn't want to miss anything.

"You need to hear this Ellie," said Naochi.

"What is that I need to hear?"

"Listen to Ben's communication channel."

After Ellie turned other channels to mute, she paid attention to Ben's communication channel. She heard some broken metallic, jumbled noises.

She turned the other channels back on.

"Analysis?" she asked.

"Nothing came out."

"These noises might be the result of the object's interference while he was inside…or might be a system malfunction."

"Please let me know when you reach a conclusion. Naochi."

In the meantime, the byxroids brought Ben and Gabriel to the mother ship. Dr. Anne and Ellie were there when they arrived. Ellie paid all her attention to them. The Byxroids undressed Ben and put him into REST rapidly to provide the nutrition his body needed and to support his body fluids. The microgravity environment's negative effects on his muscle tissues on the micro basis were recovered in the REST as well.

Ellie looked at Gabriel, who had turned into a young man. Although she didn't know why and how this happened, she wasn't questioning any more. She was lost in her memories while looking at this young face that had been a memory for her and that she had missed for years.

First analysis showed Gabriel's anatomic age as thirty-six. He was not put into REST because he didn't have genetic mutation. There was only a little swelling on his face from being in an environment where gravitation was close to zero. From a distance, the Believers were murmuring something and watching what was going on in surprise and excitement.

While Dr. Anne processed necessary medical procedure, she shared the data she obtained with everyone by simplifying it so that it could be understood.

The data coming about Gabriel's health condition was highly positive. After he was brought to the medic room, it took him thirty seconds to come to himself with Dr. Anne's intervention.

Ellie asked permission from Dr. Anne to talk to Gabriel. She accepted Ellie's request.

"How are you?" asked Ellie right after that.

"Where is the Almighty Eesho?" he asked as soon as he opened his eyes

"Is he OK?" he asked this time while he was straightening himself.

"ZA is still inside ZZ and we don't have any news from him," said Ellie.

"Ben?" asked Gabriel. "I couldn't grasp him. It's my fault, I became distracted and he-"

"Ben is here. Don't worry Gabriel," she interrupted him. "But he is still unconscious. How are you?"

"Is he here? Oh, thank God," said Gabriel. "I am fine. It's kind of weird but I feel extra ordinarily fine."

"It's nice to hear that, because we have something very important to tell you," said Ellie.

Gabriel looked at her curiously.

"Your anatomic data says you are thirty-six years old."

"What do you mean?" he asked and then he saw Avram and Nasir looking at him in amazement.

"You...You... You got younger," stuttered Avram.

Gabriel looked at his hands. His skin was tight and clear.

"How could this be?"

"We don't know," said Ellie trying to hide her excitement.

When she saw Gabriel wearing their GISSI, she had felt that they were beginning to bridge the gap between them. For years she had tried to suppress the estrangement and the rage she had felt for him for not accepting the mutation and leaving the commune. But now those feelings were gone like they had never been there before.

May be, she thought. May be the youth and the vitality he has gained will make him change his mind and accept mutation. She knew this was a small chance but seeing him changed like this gave her hope.

The Believers had surrounded Gabriel. Ellie stepped herself out of the crowd and watched them from a distance. Some were asking him how he was feeling and some were touching his youthful skin in amazement. And Gabriel, amazed with himself was telling them how wonderful he was feeling.

"This is God's grace," some said.

"God chose you to take the Almighty Eesho there and gave you your youth back because you did not question that mission," said one them.

"I'm grateful for this. Thank you, God," said Gabriel.

At that moment her reason had taken control over her emotions. Gabriel had only got younger. When she looked at his beard and long hair that she had ignored seeing moments ago now told her that they still belonged to different worlds. He wasn't any different than his fellow friends that he was talking to with sincerity now.

She left him with his friends. She was feeling guilty for what she had been thinking a while ago and went near Ben. There was something strange about Ben's condition; even though his vital signs were in stable condition, his brain wave speed was very slow. Therefore, a medical review was in process, and no change had been observed so far.

"I shouldn't have let you go there," she whispered, looking at Ben.

I was the one who said the object was coming to ZA but not to Earth. I am responsible for this. I shouldn't have sent Ben to the object. I shouldn't have paid attention to Gabriel and Ben's objections, she thought.

"This is nonsense," said Dr. Anne, interrupting Ellie's thoughts.

"What is it?" asked Ellie curiously.

"Detailed analysis cannot define his condition. There is a matter of coma but there isn't any traumatic brain injury. His vital signs are normal. There is no brain vain clot, any damage, or any brain vessel expansion or contraction. The synapses function very well, but his brain waves indicate he is in a coma."

"Why would he be in a coma with no reason and when his brain is functioning well?" asked Ellie.

"There is an unidentified problem," said Dr. Anne.

"We must apply synthesis combinations for detailed analysis," she added.

At that time, Gabriel and Ben's status reports were being evaluated in the control room.

"I am proposing the Council start running a damage detection in our community on Earth," said Diane.

"I will also propose the transfer of temporary bases in space to the main bases on the Moon and the expansion of the bases to continue without interruption. The threat continues."

While Diane and Naochi were busy doing necessary preparations and calculations, Ellie was only interested in Ben's condition. Ben's students had connected to the virtual setting of Ben's room with their PYXOMs and wanted to be there when he woke up. But they shut off their holomex images as soon as they found out about his condition from Dr. Anne's sharings.

Ellie was waiting beside Ben and there wasn't anyone else left in the room except her. Everybody seemed to have forgotten about him although he had showed so much courage and had sacrificed a lot just to stop the threat to save humanity and Earth.

"You were wrong," said Ellie to Ben, who was lying there unconsciously.

"If you were conscious now, unlike other people, you would have thought that all these had to have a meaning. Most probably, you would have started your work as soon as you returned to Earth. I think you are mistaken. You are a lot more than a historian who evaluates the past. If you were able to talk to me now, you would have inactivated all these confusions in my mind. Then you would raise your eyebrows and ask me questions when I told you we would find out the meaning behind these someday."

She paused. She thought about their life before ZA. Their plans about having a child and all those conversations they had for years. She took a deep breath.

"Understanding the past is a key to the future," she whispered. "Do you remember? I told you this when you asked me why I continued having those private conversations with you. At the time, you never asked me why I was not talking to some other historian but you. Even though you didn't ask, I should have told you why. The reason is your marvelous perspective; the way you regard things. That's why I shouldn't have let you go there."

"Do you remember the perfect universe theory? If you were conscious, we would have talked about this and you would definitely say something that would cause a flash of inspiration in my mind."

"Who knows, maybe the absolute perfection is actually the infinity itself. Perhaps the purpose of the creators of the macrocosm is to attain infinity by stopping time… The balance of the macrocosm has to be stabilized for infinity, right? For this, the time dimension has to be decelerated to the utmost… Perhaps there appears an uncalculated mistake or a chain of mistakes during this process and the creators of the macrocosm interfere at that stage. And we perceive the imperfect universe and the loop as perfect because we can evaluate the universe with our limited capacity."

"This loop might have been tested a lot of times. And we are living the same time over and over again without remembering it. In this case, if all these theories are correct, this will go on like this until the universe reaches perfection… Or perhaps each one of us is a test subject at parallel dimensions. In any case, there must be units that would check and organize the order of the universe to make sure it works properly."

"Also, there should be mechanisms to fix an error when it occurs. The things we have experienced in the last few hours must be linked to these mechanisms. But we call it 'impossible' when we encounter an event that operates against the rules and principles of the order…" Ellie paused all of a sudden. She noticed she was in the middle of a vortex of thoughts again. Then she smiled to herself as she continued.

"Maybe you can hear me right now and you are asking me, 'Haven't we talked about this today Ellie? You are right, Ben, we have. But all these incidents really have to be linked to this. I've come up against a paradox. Like I said, the laws and the regulations of the universe that restrict us will be vanished when the macrocosm attains infinity. Perhaps then humanity will have gotten the permit for an exit from this simulation loop. If we go beyond our mission, I'm afraid we have a chance of being eliminated for the next repetitive future. Therefore, this can mean as humans we might be just running around in circles for the work we did. This includes all the work and research I will do to find that factor," she said and paused. She said nothing for a while. She waited, listening to Ben's breathing.

"But," she said in a trembling voice and continued, "if you could answer me, you would have switched me away from pessimism, by telling me that we have nothing else to do but to continue exploring and trying. Wouldn't you? Maybe I am wrong about the paradox. On the contrary, maybe we were saddled with a responsibility and we have been following this path since the beginning of humanity. We are probably fulfilling the tasks we are programmed to do with minimum error. Yes, maybe that's it. Our desire to explore might be a feeling that was uploaded to us as a part of our mission. If it wasn't like this, we wouldn't have been here in this infinitive loop, right?"

"We are given limited controls now, but this doesn't mean that won't change later. Perhaps one day humanity will reach a level to determine its own future. Yes, it has got to be… I guess we react negatively like a little child when we encounter an incident that canalizes or compels us. The pessimism I am stuck with from time to time is probably because of the disappointment caused by the result of discomfort for not being able to control. And maybe we should make more effort to be virtuous about acceptance and maturity."

"If I had popularized the creator of the macrocosm, and if I was a surrender…and if I wasn't questioning this much, would this sort of acceptance be the easiest way to integrate with the creation of macrocosm in a more harmonious way?"

She hesitated and then turned her head and gazed at the Earth through the transparent walls.

"When we get back home, we will find a way to wake you up," she added in a thoughtful manner.

"We will find a way," she said still gazing at Earth.

"And as for humanity, we will also question our purpose of existence and goals once again."

Then she turned back to Ben and looked at his blank face bitterly.

"If you could answer me, you would definitely say that I was right. Isn't that correct, Ben? You would also tell me that we are at one of those crossroads as humanity… Doesn't our history tell us this anyway? Please wake up, Ben. The Earth also needs you as much as I need you."

Even though it was only one-sided long talk to Ben, this had comforted her.

CHAPTER 26

ZA had been alone inside the object, among the spheres, and left to his fate. He couldn't figure out what was happening no matter how hard he tried. He didn't have enough knowledge to analyze all these incidents. He couldn't even understand why he was experiencing these. All he remembered was his inner voice telling him to go into this strange looking gigantic object. But he didn't know why he was there either.

Then he saw a small light ball over there. The light ball started to get closer and bigger while he was trying to figure out what it was. All of a sudden, he found himself inside a hoop of light. At first his old aching eyes couldn't see anything in this brightness. But right after that, he felt a great relaxation all over his aching body. The light didn't bother his eyes anymore. He felt like he had gotten rid of a big burden; he felt himself so light and free that he could almost fly if he wanted.

While he was trying to figure out the lightness of his body, he looked at his hands instinctively. He wasn't wearing that strange outfit anymore. Also, his wrinkled, trembling hands full of dark spots had become smooth and they weren't trembling any longer. He looked down while he continued ascending. He saw a big gleaming chest. He thought it had been a while since he saw something that looked familiar to him. But when he saw his UGISSI floating close behind the chest, he directed his attention away from the chest and started concentrating on the UGISSI.

While he was watching it float in amazement, the UGISSI turned itself around and right at that moment he saw a very old man in it. He tried to focus on the UGISSI but he was really confused. That old man... Was it himself? That UGISSI was his, it had to be.

"Am I dead?" he asked himself when he saw his body moving away. Because he was driven to despair, he tried to go after his body instinctively. But shortly, the same lightness filled inside him. He was feeling so free and peaceful that his inner voice told him there was no need to go after it. He was safe.

Then he heard some voices away from him. When he carefully listened to them, the voices came closer. After that, he noticed one of the spheres coming to him at a fast speed. While it was opening up like a bowl, a bright white light appeared inside it. Right after this light surrounded him, images started to appear.

Just then, he heard a woman's voice; he remembered this sweet voice as soon as it started singing the song. This song, this voice sent a shiver down his spine.

"Mother," he said to himself.

Then he found himself in her arms, looking at her beautiful face. He was filled with peace when his mother stroked his hair affectionately.

The images around him began to disappear slowly and soon he was left with nothingness. After that, another sphere in a different size appeared before him and it opened up just like the previous one. The bright light inside it also curved before getting out. Then suddenly, ZA was surrounded with human voices. He found himself at a square in Jerusalem. Now, there were rabbis around him who listened to him with interest and respected him. He realized his voice was thinner when he was speaking. He looked at his hands and feet; how small they were. He looked at his body. He realized he was in the body of a twelve or thirteen-year-old boy.

He was puzzled. While he was looking around, the images disappeared and there was darkness again. He noticed that the huge structure he was in had shrunk. But right at that moment another sphere appeared and he concentrated on this one. Different noises and images that came from the inside of this new sphere surrounded him. He could remember now. All his memories were coming back to him while he was reliving the major chapters of his life. Now he was in the city of Galilee and he was announcing the kingdom of God and speaking himself as the son of God to the crowd. He was telling them that God had appointed him to save the poor and heal the sick people who were in pain and misery and bring happiness to all. The body he saw belonged to a male adult and his voice wasn't thin like the previous one. It was confident, merciful, and affectionate.

After another darkness, while the flickering images that came one after another were expanding and then wrapping him, he found himself in a deserted place surrounded by mountains. He was going down the hill and he could feel the burning heat of the sun. He had a suntan and was holding a stick with his dry, cracked hand.

The images changed again. This time he found himself speaking to a crowd. Then a new image came and he saw himself sitting at a dinner table. While eating, he was chatting with the people who were dining with him. After a short darkness, he found himself by the seaside. He was chatting with the fishermen, telling them why God had sent him to Earth.

Then, he found himself crucified at Golgotha hill. Below him, he saw deep sorrow, hopelessness and tears in people's eyes and heard them sobbing. He looked away from those anguished faces and looked up at the sky.

"E-LEE E-LEE L-MAA-NAA SAA-BAACH-TAA-NEE," he exclaimed.

Later, he felt that unbearable pain going away. Then he found himself in the middle of nothingness one more time. Right after that he saw himself standing by a tombstone with a cloth over it. Some people around him were gazing at him in mixed feelings, half fear and half surprise, and some were praying with their hands clasped together.

Once again, he was surrounded by the nothingness. While the silence went on, the image of the praying people disappeared and like every time a new sphere approached him, this time it was dark all over. He heard air bubbles coming out of his mouth. He opened his eyes. He was in water.

Am I drowning? he thought. When he panicked, he felt two hands lifting him up to the surface of the water. It was as if time had slowed down. Every detail began to take form in his head. All his previous experiences, everything about him, his mission, and each and every detail integrated with that slowing time gained meaning.

As soon as his head went up to the surface, he opened his eyes and saw a deep blue sky. While the soft touch of sunbeams was stroking the flowing water drops on his body, he saw a snow-white pigeon flying in the blue sky.

He looked at the man next to him; he was wearing an outfit made of sheep skin and he had a beard. He remembered it all. He smiled.

"This must be the Jordan River," he said to himself.

***

Naochi watched the last sphere in ZZ disappear. There wasn't a trace of that object now.

"Yes! Finally!" she said to herself. ZZ had become part of history.

Indicators pointed out that all conditions were positive. She reported this information on her screen to the Council. After having the information confirmed by other sources, the Council shared it with everybody in the commune. People's pessimistic expression and mood were replaced by hopefulness. Everybody was smiling now. And the Council took the positive damage report under consideration, they started a new voting for something that its results were already known;

Do you want to go back to Earth?